ENDURE THE DARKNESS

Survive the Darkness Book 11

RYAN CASEY

GET A POST APOCALYPTIC NOVEL FOR FREE

To instantly receive an exclusive post apocalyptic novel totally free, sign up for Ryan Casey's author newsletter at: ryancasey books.com/fanclub

CHAPTER ONE

Tristan Harper always thought Britain was an absolute shithole, ever since he first set foot on these shores twenty-eight long years ago.

The skies were grey. As always. Were the skies ever *not* grey in Britain? Sure, there was the occasional summer's day that everyone here went batshit crazy for. One little hint of sun, and it was barbecues out, beers out, bellies out. The smell of sweaty old men lathered in slimy sun cream. The taste of burned barbecued meat. The sound of kids shrieking. It made Tristan feel sick.

Hell. That was one thing he didn't have to worry about in a powerless world anymore. Morons getting pissed and hosting barbecues.

Except... well. They still did that in their little communities.

They still put on these false smiles and niceties whenever the sun came out.

The world had literally collapsed, and these fuckers still put everything aside for the sake of a bit of sun.

You'd really think they'd have learned by this point, wouldn't you?

He looked at the five people kneeling before him with their

hands tied behind their backs and the gags over their mouths, and he sighed. The tears on their faces. The bruises under their eyes. The smell of piss in the air from the little kid at the end with the alopecia patches, wetting himself. The sound of their desperate little whimpers. It irritated him. Not to sound unsympathetic, but it really irritated him.

And it was mostly the way they cried as if they didn't expect this that got to him most. They'd grown too comfortable in a dangerous world. Sure, fifteen years might have passed since the power fucked off and didn't come back. And years of power struggles might've followed. Power struggles over supplies. Power struggles over territory. Power struggles over frigging power struggles themselves.

And sure. A *relative* peace may have settled for a lot of communities. They had settled into a new groove. They had discovered a sense of equanimity in their lives. Accepted that power just wasn't coming back, despite the best efforts of the remaining echelons of the elite over the years.

But they had forgotten something very, very important.

It was a dangerous world out there.

And they did not have a God-given right to make it out alive.

Sad. But true.

Inevitable, even.

Tristan stood there holding on to his rifle. His hands were sweaty. Behind these five kneelers, he saw the destroyed remains of an old building. Looked like it might've been a church, once upon a time, but it was hard to tell at this point. Most of it was completely burned out from the inside. He could smell the smoke in his nostrils if he concentrated hard enough.

Hear their screams.

No! Please! Tristan! Don't do this! Don't listen to him! Don't...

He shook his head.

Pushed that thought aside.

He didn't need to think about The Moment anymore.

He'd done enough thinking about it for a lifetime at this stage.

He looked at the five before him. Looked at alopecia kid and the wet patch on his faded blue jeans. He looked at the girl by his side. Sixteen, probably. Skinny as hell. Thought she might just snap if he touched her.

He wasn't going to touch her.

He didn't want to get his hands dirty.

He looked at the three people beside her. The balding bloke with the big mole on his head and the woman with the badger-coloured hair beside him. Looked at them both and saw the way they tried to move their lips. The way the bloke cried out so much the blood vessels in his eyes looked like they'd burst completely, making them totally red.

The way he begged for his children.

And then the woman beside them both. Old woman. Staring into space. The most compliant of them all. Probably none the wiser as to what was going on.

Just staring ahead and accepting whatever fate awaited her.

Probably the best way to be.

He stood there and stared at this row of people, and he wanted to *feel* something. He wanted to *feel* guilt. He wanted to *feel* pain. He wanted to *feel* he was an absolute monster, which people would claim he was. That as much as he *knew* he was doing this for the good of all mankind and for the future of humanity... and as much as it made *sense* from a logical perspective... it was still the wrong thing to do.

Morally.

Emotionally.

But as Tristan stood there holding on to his rifle, a few specks of rain trickling down from those depressing grey skies above, staring at the family begging for their lives—begging for the lives of their children—Tristan didn't feel anything.

Coldness.

Emptiness.

A void.

He swallowed a sickly lump in his throat, and he pointed the rifle towards the mother first.

He fired.

Fired a bullet at her and watched her head snap back, heard her neck cracking.

The father cried out.

Tried to shake himself free.

Tried to lunge to his wife's side.

But then Tristan shot him too.

Watched his head explode blood and skull fragments all over the debris-laden ground.

He saw the fear in the kids' eyes, and he still didn't feel anything.

Just that, logically, he'd done the right thing by killing the parents first.

Because as traumatising as it was for a child to watch their parents die, it was far, far worse for a parent to watch their children die.

And he didn't want to traumatise anyone.

He turned the rifle at the boy next. Pointed it at him.

Saw that urine patch spreading even further across the top of his jeans.

Saw him looking right into his eyes, shaking his head.

Begging underneath that gag.

And he fired.

Shot him between the eyes.

Saw the fear and the pain and all the grief switch off in that instant.

And now it was just the girl left.

Just the girl and the old woman. Who still stared on blankly as if everything was normal. As if all was well.

He looked at the girl. Looked at her kneeling there, staring up at him.

The tears streaming waterfalls down her cheeks.

The way she shook intensely like she was having a seizure.

But also something else.

The deadness.

The dead expression in her eyes.

He looked down at her, and for a moment, for just a split second, Tristan felt something.

He felt sadness.

He felt sorrow.

He felt grief, and he felt fear.

He lifted his shaking rifle and went to pull the trigger.

Pulled it.

And then something remarkable happened.

Nothing.

Nothing at all.

No gunshot.

No blast.

Nothing.

He stood there. Totally still. Staring at the girl. Crows cawing overhead. Gunshots still echoing in his ears.

And as he stood there looking down at this girl, the bodies of her mum, dad, and brother beside her, he felt even more intensely about what he had to do.

For the first time in what felt like forever, Tristan *felt*.

He walked over to the girl.

He crouched opposite her.

Looked over his shoulder to see if anyone else was looking.

No sign of life.

All clear.

He yanked the binds free from her ankles.

And he lifted her up.

Made her stand there.

She just flopped down in a heap right away.

"Go," he said. Heart racing. Unable to understand why he was feeling so strongly suddenly. He'd done bad things. Done fucking downright awful things over the years.

Why this girl?

Why this moment?

Why now?

He grabbed her again. Lifted her to her feet. "Get up. Get up and go. Run. Run and don't look back. I don't expect you to thank me for it. But... but you have to run."

She looked up at him with this dead-eyed expression, and for a moment, he saw the woman there.

The flames.

The screams.

The baby.

The laughter.

No!

He heard movement, then.

Movement behind him.

Footsteps.

He looked back.

He couldn't see them yet. Couldn't see anybody yet.

But they were coming.

He knew they were coming.

And this girl needed to act fast if she wanted to get away.

Tristan turned around and put his hands on her bony shoulders. "Run. Run, or you're dead. Run, or they'll put you through hell. Run, or it's over. I swear to you."

He saw the way the girl looked at her grandmother.

The way her grandmother stared into the distance. Smiling. Completely vacant.

And then the girl looked back at him.

"I'm sorry," Tristan said. And he meant it. That was the weirdest thing. That was the hardest thing to understand. He *meant* his apology. "It's already too late for her."

He saw the girl shake her head. Saw her standing there in that torn white dress, her bleeding wrists still tied. He saw the purple bruises all down her luminous, pale skin, and he *felt* bad for her.

He felt the pain for what he'd done over the years.

Not just to her family.

But to everyone.

"Go," he said.

He saw her mouth utter something underneath the tape on her lips.

And then he watched her turn.

Watched her hobble away, sobbing, off into the remains of the church and out of sight.

Tristan stared off where she'd disappeared.

He stared at the derelict remains of the church.

The burned-out altar.

The cracked stained-glass window with Jesus on it.

Lord forgive me.

He looked at the old woman, staring up into the distance.

And he saw something else now.

Something different to her expression.

Her eyes didn't look vacant anymore.

They didn't look like they were smiling.

They looked... terrified.

He looked around, up the slope, and he saw exactly why.

He saw the figures standing there, looking down at him.

He saw them staring silently at him.

And for a moment, for just a moment, Tristan felt it.

Fear.

Total fear.

And then he took a deep breath, right through his nostrils, and he let that fear slip away into the air again.

He didn't feel a thing anymore.

He *couldn't* feel a thing anymore.

That was life now.

CHAPTER TWO

Billy felt the splitting agony in the centre of his palms, and he knew today would be a long one.

He walked down the street and prayed nobody saw him. It was another warm day. A little hazy and a gentle breeze, which felt nice. He could hear the birds singing, one of his favourite noises. A reminder of how to aspire to be, in a way.

Birds didn't care about the lack of electricity or power. They didn't care about food or water shortages.

They just lived entirely in the present and got on with their lives.

He figured he and the rest of his species could learn a lot from them.

He walked down the cracked pavement towards the end of the street and bit his lip. That throbbing pain in his hands wasn't getting any better. Damn it. He'd had them re-stitched and re-bandaged a couple of weeks ago now. And it was three months since he'd had a pair of nails hammered through them by that lunatic leader of the Animals, Wolf.

So why was he still in so much pain?

He closed his eyes as he walked and tried to lean into the pain rather than push it away. A trick Steve taught him once. Resisting pain always made it worse, without fail. Because by *resisting* it, you're adding another layer of suffering on top of the suffering you're already experiencing.

But by accepting it... by leaning into it and allowing it to sit there... you were just experiencing the pain or the suffering as raw data, nothing more, nothing less.

Okay. Nice idea in principle.

But in practice, very bloody difficult.

He was in agony. And it wasn't easing off at all. And no mental tricks could do a thing to change that.

He took deep breaths of the warm summer air as he walked down the pavement. He could smell cut grass. The warm tarmac of the road. And that weird, fresh smell that always accompanied a warm day. You know the one. Hard to put your finger on it exactly, but it always reminded you of being a kid. The freshness of the sun against the leaves of the trees.

The memory of childhood summers.

Of holidays.

Of happiness.

But as much as Billy tried to distract himself with the buffet of sensory experiences all around him, it was pointless. Totally fucking pointless.

The pain in his palms was so bad, he felt like he might actually vomit.

Which would be a fucking disaster for more reasons than he cared to explain.

Vomiting on the job?

Vomiting on the job in front of Marco?

Vomiting on the job in front of Marco and Jorah?

Vomiting on the job in front of Marco and Jorah and Faye?

He shuddered at the thought.

He was very, very keen not to suffer complete social death today.

So what did he do?

Go back home? Go down to Doctor Khaleed's to see why this might be happening?

No. Of course he didn't.

He just kept on walking. Didn't need to go giving Jorah any reason to fire him. He was lucky enough to get the job in the first place, especially after his injuries only three months ago. He wasn't going to let any little bit of pain snatch it from him.

He gritted his teeth and stared at the wall ahead, towering twenty feet above. As much as the attitude around Eastbrook was very much a "build bridges, not walls" kind of vibe, the incident with the Animals and Jarrod's people three months ago was enough to panic people here into constructing some kind of safe measures. Resistances of some sort.

Because as much as Billy had been well aware that they didn't live in a kumbaya, sing around the fireplace, hippy-dippy world, there were plenty of people here who had forgotten that there was a dangerous world out there. And that as much as they hated to admit it, there were folks out there who wished their people harm.

And because of that, one of the first decisions was to construct walls around the community.

There was some pushback from a few residents. Especially those who lived closest to the proposed walls. They worried about the lack of light to their houses or about the noise from the increased guard presence. There'd been smaller entrance points and fencing for a while of course, but nothing on this scale.

But honestly, hearing people kick off about the wall impacting their view was kind of reassuring.

Because it proved that most people really had accepted the world they were living in now.

Nothing like a bit of superficial bitching to remind you of your innate humanity, right?

He saw the wall up ahead, the sun beating down on his head, and he felt sick.

Sick, as the throbbing pain in his hands grew progressively worse, gradually more intense.

As he started to grow dizzy.

He thought of what Marco and the thugs he hung around with would say if they saw him struggling.

Shook his head.

Come on, Billy. Hold it together. Hold your shit together...

He walked another few steps down the pavement when suddenly he heard a voice behind him.

"Hi, Billy."

He froze. Stopped dead in his tracks.

His stomach sank.

Because he knew who that voice belonged to.

He knew very damned well who that voice belonged to.

His heart raced. His head throbbed. His face grew hotter and hotter as beads of sweat trickled from his armpits.

He turned around slowly and saw her standing right there on the pavement.

Faye was gorgeous. Make no mistake about it. Those long, slender legs. Those glistening green eyes. And that understated smile.

She waved at him. "Hi."

Billy fancied Faye. Which sounded an utterly ridiculous thought for a mid-twenties man, he realised. But the blackout had kind of done a number on people's emotional maturity and intelligence, which was surely totally understandable.

He'd been trying to get closer to Faye for the three months since the conflict with the Animals.

Trying to get to know her.

Trying to make *himself* feel more comfortable around her.

But you know what?

All those efforts had been pretty fucking futile.

"You okay?" Faye asked. He saw her smile drop. Saw those eyes of hers widen. "You look... kind of pale."

Kind of pale.

Shit.

He couldn't go making her think he was a freak.

He had to do something.

He had to show he was okay.

Show he was fine.

He lifted his right hand and started to wave.

The throbbing pain in his palm changed from a dull ache to a sharp, intense stab, right down his forearm, up towards his shoulder, and then into his throat, and...

He couldn't stop himself.

Oh fuck, he couldn't stop himself...

He tasted the stomach acid in his mouth.

And as much as he told himself—ordered himself—to keep his shit together, he couldn't help vomiting it all out on the pavement before him.

He crouched with his hands to his knees. Stomach aching. Entire body on fire.

He looked up at Faye's shocked face as a chunk of vomit clung to his chin.

"I don't... I don't feel too good," he said.

And then suddenly, the dizziness took over completely, and Billy fell to the ground in a haze of shame, embarrassment, and total fucking agony.

CHAPTER THREE

"Billy? You okay? He's awake. I—I think he's awake. Billy?"

Billy opened his eyes. He felt groggy as hell. Everything around him looked hazy, and he couldn't see properly. Shit. Where the hell was he? What the fuck had happened?

And was that *Faye's* voice he could hear?

"Are you okay, Billy? You fell pretty bad. And your hands..."

His hands.

Shit.

The second Faye mentioned his hands, he felt himself transported back.

Walking down the street in the blistering summer sun.

The agony shooting right up his arms and right down his spine.

Making him puke right in front of Faye.

Puking, then collapsing.

He tried not to think about it. Tried to erase that memory from his mind, to save himself from the embarrassment.

But there was no hiding from that memory.

Or from the embarrassment.

He lay there on his back, wherever he was right now. His cheeks burned. He could hear muffled voices. His head ached. He could taste vomit at the back of his throat, too, which made him feel even lousier, even more sickly.

He didn't want to open his stinging eyes. He wanted to stay hidden and protected by the darkness of oblivion.

But in the end, he knew he had no choice.

He opened his eyes.

This time, the figures around him weren't as blurry. He could see Faye at his right, staring down at him. She was holding on to his arm, which was more uncomfortable than Billy wanted to admit in front of Faye. He'd already bloody embarrassed himself in front of her enough today. Didn't want to go making himself look even more of a wimp.

"Billy," Faye said, a smile flickering across her face. "You're awake. Are you okay?"

Billy looked up at Faye, and for a moment, for just a damned moment, he felt quite flattered that she seemed so concerned about him. Maybe vomiting all over your shoes then passing out in agony in the middle of the street was exactly the sort of maverick move Billy had been waiting for to finally win her affections all along.

But then he saw they weren't alone.

Marco was at his left side, staring down at him.

Marco looked happy to see Billy in a different way. He looked *happy*, no doubt about that, with that frigging smirk across his face.

But of course he was happy. Because he hated Billy. He'd hated him ever since Connor and the rest of that gang were killed by Jarrod's people three months ago—and probably hated him longer than that, too.

Basically, he was probably the last person Billy wanted by his bedside right now.

He looked around the room he was in. Little office area with a bed in the middle. The surgery. Makeshift hospital. Shit. He must've passed out real bad if he'd had no memory of being carried along this way.

"We were worried about you," Faye said. "You really didn't look well. And then you vomited everywhere, and... and then you passed out. Right in front of us."

Billy swallowed a sickly lump in his throat. "I... I think I was just hot."

"Pissed yourself a little, too," Marco said, with those mock pity in his voice. He tilted his head, tried his best not to smile. "All over your jeans. But don't worry. We put you another pair on while you were asleep."

He patted Billy on his shoulder, which made him wince with agony.

"Oh, sorry," Marco said. "I forgot. The hands."

"My hands... my hands are fine," Billy said.

"Fine?" Marco said. "Really? They don't look fine to me."

"I... I just slipped earlier and hurt them a bit, that's all. But it's really not so bad. I... I need to get up. I need to get to work."

He tried dragging himself off the bed. He needed to get the hell out of here before he either passed out again or ended up punching Marco in his damned smug face.

But as he tried to stand, he realised just how dizzy he was. And just how grim he felt.

"Woah," Faye said. "You need to sit down, Billy. Lie down."

"I can't just lie down in here."

"You've passed out," Faye said. "And you don't look well at all. The best thing you can do for yourself right now is take it as easy as possible."

"Yeah," Marco said. "You don't want to go throwing up and pissing yourself again, do you?"

"Marco," Faye said, rolling her eyes.

Marco raised his hands. "I'm deadly serious. Like, nobody on the team wants to see you piss yourself on the job. Especially not me."

Billy stared into his eyes and did his very best not to take a swing at him. But it was proving very fucking difficult.

"Look," Billy said, turning to Faye. "I appreciate you... I appreciate you bringing me here. I don't know what happened. But really. I'm fine now. I need to get to work. I'm absolutely fine. A funny turn, that's all it is. If I can get to work, then I'm sure I'll feel a hell of a lot better than if I spend another second in here."

"You sure about that, Billy?" Marco said. "See, I really think I should stick around at least. Just in case you shit yourself this time. I really, really wouldn't want to miss that. For your sake, of course."

Billy turned around to Marco and narrowed his eyes.

He could take his neck off his shoulders if his hands weren't wounded.

If he wasn't a fucking cripple, he could do real damage to this piece of shit.

But he *was* a fucking cripple.

And there was no getting away from that.

He took a breath, turned away from Marco, and back to Faye.

"I appreciate it. Seriously. But I'm gonna get out of here now and get to work."

"There'll be no need for that."

A voice.

Not Marco's voice.

A deeper voice.

A voice that filled him with fear.

He looked around, and he saw Jorah, the leader of Eastbrook, standing there.

Arms folded in front of his body.

Long white beard trailing in front of his arms.

Staring at Billy like he was some alien who'd just crash-landed from another planet.

"Marco, Faye? You make yourself scarce. Billy and I have some talking to do."

Billy saw Marco's smirk widen as he walked over to the door, Faye by his side.

"Good luck," Marco muttered.

And then he walked out of there, leaving Billy alone with Jorah.

Good luck.

Marco was right.

Billy was going to need it.

CHAPTER FOUR

At the top of Billy's list today was certainly not a chat with fucking Jorah.

Fucking Jorah, as Billy now referred to him, mostly in his head and to Steve, was the leader of Eastbrook. He wasn't a bad guy. Honestly, for the most part, he was really a rather decent guy.

But he and Billy had history. He'd never particularly liked Billy all that much. Probably because Billy saw through his egotistical bullshit. He was the "de facto leader" of Eastbrook, and boy did he like to remind you of that fact. Not in a violent way or anything. Not in a "salute the fuck out of me then get down on your knees and let me come inside you" way.

But in a way, that actually annoyed Billy more. Wandering around waving at people like he was some kind of fucking local celebrity. Which he sort of was. And in a world where celebrities were basically non-existent, there would always be one wanker taking full advantage of that fact.

But yeah. Sitting opposite him in this dingy little makeshift hospital room was definitely not where Billy wanted to be right now.

"Billy," Jorah said, sounding just as jovial as ever. "How are we doing?"

How are we doing? That was something else this bastard always said. How are *we* doing. As if whoever Jorah was talking to had some kind of hive-mind connection with him.

And Billy knew it always preceded something, too. Usually something bad.

Which was why it was more important than ever that Billy got the hell out of this conversation ASAP.

"Good. I was just heading to work, actually. Just had a funny turn this morning, that's all. Anyway. Nice to see you. I'd best be off—"

"Actually, Billy, that's not going to be necessary."

Oh, shit. There it was. Diversion attempt well and truly foiled.

And now here he stood, looking this bastard in the eye as he stared back at him like a disappointed headteacher, and for what?

Because he'd had a funny turn?

Because he was in pain but still willing to work anyway?

"Billy," Jorah said. "Get back in bed. Please."

"Wow," Billy said. "Not what I expected."

"What?"

"I mean... I've seen the way you look at me. But you could at least ask me out on a date first."

Jorah narrowed his eyes like he didn't understand. Sense of humour really was lost on him.

"Please," Jorah said. "It'd make me feel a whole lot more relaxed if you could relax."

"And it would make me feel a whole lot more relaxed if you let me do what I want to do to relax."

"What are you even saying?"

"Honestly, I'm not entirely sure at this point. But... but what is this about?"

Damn. He wished he'd never asked. Wished he'd never given

Jorah an opportunity to air whatever grievances he had. He couldn't possibly roast him for anything here, could he? He'd just passed out. His hands were in pain, serious pain. Surely now wasn't the time or the place?

Jorah sighed. "I really don't want to have to do this. Especially not now."

Oh. Oh, shit. He really was going there. He really was doing "this", whether he wanted to or not. Whatever "this" was."

"No," Billy said.

Jorah frowned. "What?"

"Sorry. I guess... I'm just thinking aloud. What?"

Jorah sighed. Scratched his head. And at that moment, as his fingers brushed across his grey, dandruff laden mane, Billy pictured all the possibilities. He was going to fire him from his job because he was completely incompetent. He was going to amputate his hands because he didn't like the look of them. He was going to get him on his knees and...

Shit. What was with all the getting on the knees today?

"I'm retiring, Billy. I'm stepping down. And... and after what happened three months ago, with the Animals and the one you called Jarrod... and the way things were handled... well, I'm starting to think you might well be the best person to run this place."

Billy snorted. Actually snorted. Holy shit. Where the hell had that come from? He definitely hadn't been expecting that one.

"Wait," Billy said. "What? Leader? Retiring? Me?"

"I know this is a lot to dump on you, especially when you've had a turn today. But the truth is... I'm dying, Billy."

Billy frowned. Shook his head. "Wait. That can't be—"

"I was diagnosed with pancreatic cancer right before the power went out. I was told I probably had six months to live, and the second I started vomiting and suffering diarrhoea, the second I started withdrawing and losing my energy, then I probably was reaching the end.

"Somehow, I survived this long. There was a slim chance, apparently. A miracle. And I've been grateful for it. Very grateful for the extra years I've had. Tumultuous as they have been. But I'm... I'm reaching the end, Billy. I know it. I can feel it in my bones. I don't have long left. Everything the doctor told me I'd experience within six months, I'm experiencing now. And I know I need to see someone in place to be the custodian of Eastbrook before I go. It's... it's my dying wish."

Billy sat totally still. He didn't know what to say. What the fuck *was* there to say? Jorah was dying. He was dying and maybe wasn't as much of an arsehole as Billy painted him as.

But not only that. He was dying, and he wanted Billy to take over as leader of this place.

How?

How in hell had this happened?

"Sorry," Jorah said, waving a hand. "I realise this really was not ideal timing."

"No," Billy said. "I just... I don't know what to say, really."

Jorah smirked. Shit, he really did look ill, come to think of it. Pale as a ghost. "You could keep things simple and say 'yes'?"

Billy legitimately did not know what to say. What could you possibly say when someone told you they were probably dying of cancer imminently *and* wanted you to take over as community leader, especially when you didn't even think the bloke asking you this really liked you all that much?

"I mean, I'll... I just don't understand."

Jorah shuffled on the spot. "You see, pancreatic cancer can be—"

"Not about the cancer. Which I am sorry about, by the way. Really. I just... Why me?"

Jorah looked deeply into his eyes now, in a way that made him feel quite violated and uncomfortable. "I haven't always liked you."

"Surprise admission of the year."

"But I've always respected you. And I've always seen something in you. Which is why when you've fallen short of those expectations, I've always been disappointed in you. Not because I'm being an arsehole, Billy. But because you've fallen short of my hopes for you. And for the future of this place. But today..."

He gasped. Held his stomach. Went a nasty shade of green.

"Are you... are you okay?"

Jorah waved him off. "I'm... I'm as fine as can be. But as you can see. I'm going to need an answer soon."

Billy really didn't know what the hell to say. He'd just woken up after passing out. And he was in agony himself. Definitely underprepared for this. "I mean... I mean I'm going to have to think about it."

Jorah nodded. But he looked disappointed. "Time isn't exactly a luxury for me. But I understand."

All kinds of things spiralled around Billy's mind. What would leadership entail? Wouldn't there need to be an election?

And again, why the hell would Jorah choose him of all people as his successor, really, and not someone he liked more?

"Get home," Jorah said. "Get some rest. Get yourself cleaned up. And think about it. You know where I'll be. Exactly where I'll be. For how long, I can't make any promises. But for a little longer, I'll be there. Long enough to nominate you if you choose this path. Which will bypass the need for an election. For another two years, anyway."

Billy stood opposite Jorah, still speechless. At the start of this conversation, he was fully expecting to lose his job and be humiliated in front of the man he hated, Marco, and the woman he had a mad crush on, Faye.

Instead, he was being nominated as Jorah's successor.

"Think about it," Jorah said, hobbling out of the hospital room, trying to stand tall. "But Billy?"

Billy nodded. "What?"

"Wipe that undigested piece of carrot from your chin, please. That's really not the look of a leader in making."

CHAPTER FIVE

"Let me get this straight. Jorah's dying. And not only that, but he asked *you* to take over as leader?"

The surprise and amazement in Steve's voice echoed Billy's thoughts exactly. Not to mention how a smile kept breaking at the corner of his lips. He thought Billy was taking the piss; that much was clear. Thought this was some kind of weird joke.

And honestly, Billy was beginning to wonder the same.

"Seriously, I'm as surprised as you are," Billy said.

Steve sat opposite Billy in his back garden. Gorgeous day. Warmest Billy could remember—and that was saying a lot because it'd been one bloody warm summer.

He could hear the birds singing above. Hear a few lads kicking a football around on the street out front. Somewhere in the distance, he could hear the murmur of voices from the construction site, where Billy should be right now, helping build that wall.

Instead, here he was. Sitting in Steve's back garden. Beer in hand.

Trying to wrap his head around this morning's events.

"Trust me," Steve said, sipping his beer. "There's no frigging way you're anywhere near as surprised as I am."

"Charming," Billy said. "Shows a lot of faith. I appreciate that."

"It's not that," Steve said. "It's just... Well. First, I hear you're passing out. Then you're telling me Jorah's not got long to live. And that he wants *you* to follow in his footsteps."

"That's pretty much exactly it, yeah."

Steve shook his head. Puffed out his lips. "Just a lot to take in, y'know?"

"Tell me about it," Billy said.

He stroked Rex, who lay at his feet. Fat lump barely moved these days. He was old. Very old. And it was quite common for Billy to be certain he was dead at last, only for the mutt to wag that docked little tail.

He was a good dog. He'd been a good companion over the years.

And he reminded him of Aoife. Of Kayleigh.

Of the people who shaped him.

He knew he didn't have long left. But there was no sadness at that thought. Well, obviously a little. But more than anything, a sense of gratitude. He felt so lucky to have been able to spend so many years with Rex. So lucky to have a friend like him.

When the day came that Rex passed on into whatever doggy heaven awaited him, at least he'd know he gave him the best life he possibly could.

"Are you sure this actually happened?" Steve asked.

"What?"

"This whole Jorah telling you you're gonna be leader thing."

"What point are you actually making?"

Steve shrugged. "I mean, you passed out, didn't you? You sure you didn't dream it? Or bump your head or summat?"

Billy sighed. "I passed out because... because I don't know. People pass out sometimes."

"You passed out because you've been taking too bloody much on."

"I haven't been taking too bloody much on."

"You bloody have. I don't mean to be a party pooper, but those hands of yours had two nails ploughed through the middle of 'em. Even I can see the pain it causes you to just walk from A to B. Let alone construction work."

Billy shook his head. "They're really not as bad as they—agh."

"Oh, they're really not as bad as they 'agh' are they?"

"I just... I had a bad morning, that's all. But I'm fine now. Well. Fine, but with the prospect of leading an entire community staring me in the face."

"So you're thinking about it?" Steve asked.

Billy sighed. Truth be told, no. He couldn't think of anything worse. He didn't want to be leader of this place or these people. He just wanted to live the life he'd been living for the past few months. He'd been here ten years now, but the last few months since the attacks had been better. He'd felt more connected with the community. Felt more accepted by people here.

But leading them?

No. That wasn't a road he wanted to go down.

Was it?

"I just... I feel like there's far better options than me."

"Probably right."

"You're supposed to say, 'I'm sure that's not true, son'."

"Didn't you get the memo? I'm not that kind of dad."

Billy shook his head, smirked a little. "No. I suppose you're not."

Steve leaned forward then. "Look, Billy. Whatever you decide... I've got your back, okay? Sometimes leaders aren't the ones you expect. Sometimes the best leaders are the ones who were picked last at football in school. Because they're the ones who are willing to let things play out but ain't afraid to step in if there is trouble. Whatever you decide... I've got your back. It won't be easy. And you'll need all the friends you can get. But I've got your back."

"Wow," Billy said.

"What?"

"Just then, I think something happened. I think you just gave me a pep talk."

Steve scoffed. "I'm trying to be supportive here, kid."

"Yeah, well, don't quit the day job. Which you've already quit. But you get my point. And besides. I never got picked last at football."

Steve raised an eyebrow.

"Okay. Maybe I got picked next to last at football. Some of the time."

He looked around the garden. Looked at the backs of these terraced houses. He listened to the laughter on the street outside. The construction noise.

And he felt that twinge of pain in the middle of his palms, gnawing at him like a toothache.

And that prompted something else.

Memories.

Memories of the darkness.

Memories of the pain.

Memories of the warm whispers on his neck and the cold hands on his skin.

Memories he'd tried to push away for so many years.

"I appreciate Jorah's offer. And what you said. But no."

"No, what?" Steve asked.

"I can't be leader of this place. I just... I just can't. It has to go to election. Someone better and more qualified than I am has to stand. It can't be me."

He looked around at Steve, sitting there in the sunlight, and he swore he saw disappointment in his eyes.

"Whatever you decide, kid. Whatever you decide."

Billy nodded. He knew what his decision was. He knew he absolutely couldn't take the role of leader.

He took a sip of his beer and felt the bubbles popping in his mouth.

Felt the warmth of the sun.

And the pain in his hands growing stronger and stronger...

He wasn't going to be leader of this place.

He wasn't the one to succeed Jorah.

Out of nowhere, a storm cloud emerged, and thunder began to rumble.

CHAPTER SIX

Billy was back in the garage again.

His hands were tied behind his back. His wrists were bound so tightly together that one small move felt like it would burst the contents of his fingers all over the place. It was dark. Not just night-time dark, but darker than that. The deepest black you can ever possibly imagine, toned down by a thousand.

And it was the thought of what might hide in that darkness that really made him shudder.

He tried to turn his head to scan the room, but he couldn't move a muscle. He could smell something in the air. Shit. Piss. Sweat. Vomit. A horrible concoction of all those things.

And then he realised the smells were probably coming from him.

He sat there on this damp floor. He couldn't see it, but he knew the floor. He knew the garage. He'd been here plenty of times. More times than he could remember.

Every single night for the past ten years of his life—and beyond.

He tried to move his legs. Tried to stand. Heart thumping so fast he could hear it echoing around his skull, bouncing off the distant walls of this dark garage.

But he wasn't strong enough to move.

He was never strong enough to move.

"Billy."

He heard the whisper right behind him, and it turned his skin cold. His heart raced faster. He knew it was impossible. There was a wall behind him. There was no way anyone could be behind him.

And yet...

He felt something on the back of his neck. Something that made the hairs there stand right on end.

Breathing.

Warm breathing, right against his skin.

His stomach sank. His heart beat faster and faster.

They were here.

They were here, just like they were always here.

And there was no escaping them.

There was no getting away from them.

"Billy!"

A shout, this time. Right in his ear.

Making him jump out of his skin.

Heart racing so fast he was pretty sure he might have a heart attack.

Fear paralysing him, rooting him to the spot.

And then the fingers.

The icy fingers, right against the back of his neck.

Cold.

Slimy.

Dripping saliva.

Dripping blood.

"It's okay," a man's voice said. Calm. Soft. "You don't have anything to worry about. I'm here. Daddy's here. Daddy's gonna look after you, sweetie..."

He heard those words and felt those cold fingers and the warm breaths against the back of his neck, and he wanted to disappear.

He wanted to hide in that void he went to whenever this happened.

The place where he didn't hear the voices or the grunts.

The place where he didn't feel their cold hands or their sweaty bodies.

The place where—

"BILLY!"

He opened his eyes and jolted upright in his bed.

He sat there. Sweating. Shaking. Crying. Heart beating just as fast as it was in the dream.

Just a dream, Billy. Just a dream…

He covered his face with his shaking hands, and he cried. He kept on telling himself the dreams would get better over time. That the dreams would pass, and he'd move on from everything that'd happened in his childhood.

He kept on telling himself to hold those thoughts back.

Or to *accept* them. To accept them and let them in…

But no.

There was no accepting those memories.

There was no letting them in.

There was only pushing them down and holding them back.

Drowning them.

He sat there on his bed. He felt cold. His heart was still hammering away. He breathed in and out through his nostrils as he sat there.

Dad.

Murdering the man he'd called Dad.

Mum…

"No," he muttered.

He climbed out of bed. That was the only thing for it. Keep busy. The only solution.

Distract himself.

Distract himself from the memories.

Distract himself from the pain.

He walked past Rex, who didn't move a muscle.

Walked down the hallway towards the bathroom.

Opened the bathroom door, stepped inside, and lit a candle right by the mirror.

He stared at himself in the mirror. At the bags under his eyes. His hairline, receding just a little. Those greys in his curly fringe. The little patch on the right of his otherwise perfect beard.

He looked into his eyes, and he wondered why these memories were only just resurfacing.

Why he'd successfully been able to hold them back for so many years, only for them to catch up with him now.

He felt them stalking him.

Felt them following him.

Felt them sneaking up on him...

And then he remembered what Jorah said.

About wanting him to be the leader of this place.

He heard those words in his head, and he remembered, beneath the bemusement, there was something else he'd felt.

Pride.

Pride that Jorah saw something in him.

And then the memories resurfaced, his past actions resurfaced, and he didn't feel pride anymore.

He felt shame.

Dirty shame.

He opened the bathroom mirror.

Reached in there for the screwdriver.

Knowing full well this wasn't good.

Knowing full well that this was the main reason he'd been in so much pain lately.

But knowing full well that this was the only way to fight his way past the memories.

To distract himself.

He untied his bandage from his left hand.

Looked down at the scar, right in the middle of his palm.

Swallowed a lump in his throat.

And then he buried that screwdriver into his palm.

A bolt of pain, like lightning, through his body.

A blitz of sheer agony.

But amidst that agony... silence.

Total silence.

He held the screwdriver against his aching, burning palm, and amid pain, Billy felt the memories fading.

He felt his past creeping away, back into those darkened shadows.

He felt contentment.

CHAPTER SEVEN

Jorah opened his eyes and knew somebody was in his house.

It was late. Early hours of the morning, actually. It was quiet outside. But then again, Jorah never knew perfect silence. He'd suffered with tinnitus for as long as he could remember. He used to think it was just the way everyone experienced the world until he was told by a doctor that it absolutely wasn't.

And once the doctor pointed that out to him, it was impossible to take his mind off.

Good job the doctor broke the news he had pancreatic cancer the same day, or tinnitus really might've wrecked his life.

He chuckled to himself, and it hurt. He felt tired. Exhausted. He always did these days. The pain in the middle of his torso grew more intense by the day. He didn't like getting up from bed anymore. Didn't have the energy to get through a day.

He just wanted to lie in bed and sleep.

He knew the day was approaching that he wouldn't wake up from that sleep, though.

The day where the great wave of darkness would crash over him and drag him under, once and for all.

Jorah sighed. He knew he shouldn't feel sorry for himself. He'd had a good life. He was in his seventies, so he could hardly complain about his innings.

But then, no number of years on this earth was ever enough, was it?

He heard the footsteps creaking around downstairs, and he swallowed a lump in his dry throat.

He stared across his bedroom at the door. Listened to those footsteps climbing up the stairs. Whoever it was, they were making no secret about their presence. Why would they? He was a weak old man at this point, and as much as he tried to put on a stronger front, he knew plenty of people saw past it.

He gulped again. He felt sickly, so sickly. There was a smell of vomit in the air, a smell that seemed to cling to him these days. No amount of expensive aftershave could mask that stench.

He was in his final weeks. Or his final days. It was happening exactly as the doctor told him it would all those years ago. Just a lot later than he told him it would. Six months, he gave him. Six damned months to live. Being told something like that does a real number on you, that's for sure. Alters your perspective in a way that's totally unimaginable.

At first, fear. Existential dread. Thinking about what you were doing six months ago and how you'll be doing nothing at all in six months' time.

And then... a weird sense of peace. Of contentment. A recognition of the beauty in the world around you.

Gratitude.

Pure gratitude.

And as those footsteps got further up his stairs, reaching the top floor, he felt a tear roll down his cheek. Tasted it, salty on his lips.

Had he lived the life he wanted to lead?

He thought about Hilda, his wife. He thought about how they'd never been able to bring a child into this world. He thought about the strain it caused between them. He thought about the arguments. The threats to leave.

He thought about their imperfectly beautiful marriage, and he had no regrets about anything.

He thought about the day he'd held her hand as she died. Three weeks after the blackout. No access to her heart medication, which she relied on to survive.

"Never thought you'd be the one to outlive me," she said.

The final words she said to him.

And then, non-existence.

He took a deep breath as those footsteps crept closer to his bedroom door.

As they stopped, just outside.

And behind that door, he pictured Death himself.

Holding on to his scythe.

Eternal smile etched on his skeletal face.

Have you lived the life you wanted to lead?

Do you have no regrets?

He swallowed another lump in his throat and watched that door open.

He saw someone standing there.

But it wasn't Death.

It was somebody else.

"You," Jorah said.

The figure walked across the bedroom.

Walked right over to his side.

Stood there, right over him, and looked down at him, pity in their eyes.

"I didn't expect you," he said.

They looked right down into his eyes.

Stroked his clammy forehead with their slender fingers.

"I'm sorry it has to be this way."

And then he saw the blade, but it was already too late to do anything about it, too late to fight, as they lifted that blade and buried it in his chest, and then his stomach, and as he lay there being stabbed again and again and again, as he felt the agony taking over and tasted and smelled the blood, it was the cancer he thought of. He wondered if they'd hit his pancreas, wondered if they'd pierced the tumour, wondered if they'd kept him alive, wondered if...

More stabbing.

More pain.

And then that figure looking down at him again.

Blood trickling from the knife.

A chunk of flesh dangling from a string of innards.

"I'm sorry," they said.

And they meant it.

Jorah could tell they really meant it.

Jorah tried to open his mouth.

He tried to speak.

But he knew his moment had arrived.

He knew Death was finally here.

"Whatever you do..." he started.

But he didn't finish.

Blood filled his throat and seeped out of his mouth.

He tried to breathe, but he couldn't, not anymore.

He lay there in the darkness, and he felt like he was back in that doctor's surgery again, being given the diagnosis.

First, the fear.

The panic.

The dread.

And then...

And then, out of nowhere, from somewhere deep within...

The peace.

Total peace.

CHAPTER EIGHT

Billy crouched opposite Aoife's tree and waited for her to give him some clarity or some guidance.

It was morning. He hadn't slept much last night. But that was okay. The pain in his hands was enough to distract him from the thoughts. Whenever he *did* slip off into sleep, it wasn't for long enough to fall into a nightmare. To fall into that dark garage. To feel the cold, icy hands against his thighs. Or to feel the warmth of that smelly breath against his face, panting, panting, panting...

Or to remember...

No.

No, he didn't have to remember that.

He didn't have to go there.

He'd got up as soon as he saw the sun rising and as soon as the pain started to wear off and headed out into the woods. It was a nice day again. Yesterday's storm clouds seemed to have passed over, and the gorgeous summer they'd all been enjoying at Eastbrook was back in full flow.

He sat opposite Aoife's tree now. The one he'd decided would be her memorial tree all those years ago. He wasn't sure why he'd chosen this tree. Not really. He figured the way the branches stretched around and twisted around the bark made it kind of unique, and he liked it.

It brought him comfort somehow. A weird tradition, he knew.

But it'd brought him a lot of clarity over the years.

He just wished it'd bring him some serious clarity right now.

He looked at the tree and took deep breaths of the warm summer morning air. The ground was still covered in dew, cool against his fingertips. Birdsong all around him, and the sound of the leaves rustling against one another. Perfect silence here. Perfect solitude. A place he could come to when he needed clarity. When he needed peace of mind.

When he needed hope.

He looked at the tree and waited for it to speak to him. Waited for *her* to speak to him. Not literally. It was a fucking tree. He wasn't insane.

But... you know. *Emotionally*, he figured. That's how it spoke to him. Some people have meditation. Some people have prayer.

Billy's way was sitting in front of a tree and waiting for it to communicate with him.

Don't ever call him a fucking weirdo.

"He asked me to be leader," Billy said.

He could picture Aoife raising her eyebrow in bemusement, just like Steve had.

"Yeah. I thought you might react that way."

He sat there and looked across the woods. Looked at the trees. Looked at the sunlight peeking through the branches towards the ground.

"What do you think? A bizarre suggestion, right?"

No response.

Of course, there was no response.

He thought of the dreams. Of the nightmares.

And he thought of the pain.

"The weird thing is... I felt proud. For a second. When he

asked me. I felt like... like yeah. Like I could be leader. Proud that he'd think that of me. Kind of emotional. But then I remembered why I can't be anything like that. Because... because of what happened to me. Because of who I am. Because of the things I've done."

The sickly taste of another person's sweat on his lips.

The stinging pain on his backside after being slapped.

The sound of them laughing at him...

All of it just made him feel this shame.

This deep, deep sense of shame over who he was.

Over the things he'd done.

"Someone like me can't be a leader," Billy said. "Because a leader needs to be... a leader needs to have their shit together. And honestly, I'm not sure I do. Not anymore."

He looked at the tree. Looked at the pale brown bark. Looked at those twisted branches. Listened to the green leaves rustling against each other above.

"Look at me," Billy said. "Having a chat with a bloody tree. And expecting some kind of profound answer. And here I am wondering whether I'm in a good enough place mentally to consider actually leading..."

He trailed off because he heard something.

Footsteps.

Footsteps in the woods, over to his right.

He squinted into the woods. Towards the trees. And he remembered that day three months ago.

The day Jarrod's people emerged from nowhere.

The way they attacked and slaughtered Connor and so many others.

He felt the hairs on the back of his neck standing on end.

A shiver down his spine.

No. That was then, and this is now.

You're okay now. You're going to be okay.

He looked back at Aoife's tree, and he noticed something there on the bark.

Blood.

Blood trickling to the lush green grass below.

He blinked, and suddenly when he looked again, the blood was gone.

There was no blood there.

He swallowed a lump in his throat, and he stood.

He looked around the woods.

Looked at the trees.

Listened to the breeze.

The birds were silent now.

The wind, gradually easing...

Everything so quiet.

But that unshakable feeling he was being watched.

He looked at Aoife's tree, and he knew she'd seen what he'd seen.

The memories.

The thoughts.

Pouring out of his mind and to the surface...

A taste of vomit in his mouth.

He swallowed it down.

Swallowed it down and hoped the surfacing thoughts followed it as he picked at the holes in his palms.

And then he turned around, and he walked away.

He needed to get back home.

He needed to get away from here.

He needed to get to safety.

If only he knew what was waiting for him.

CHAPTER NINE

When Billy got back to Eastbrook, he knew immediately that something was wrong.

He just couldn't put his finger on what it was.

He walked down the main street towards Jorah's place. His turn in the woods had solidified his decision. There was no way he could accept Jorah's offer of leadership.

He wasn't the man for the job. He wasn't cut out for it. Not even slightly.

It needed to be someone else.

But as he walked down the sunny road, there was a little sense of disappointment deep inside. Disappointment in himself.

Because a part of him *wanted* to accept that offer.

A part of him *wanted* to believe he could lead this place.

A part of him was flattered. Truly flattered.

But his most prevailing feeling right now was one of shame.

A sense of inevitability.

The role of leadership would never be for him.

Not with the memories he had.

Not with the feelings he had...

He squeezed his fists just tight enough to send two shooting pains right up his arms.

Don't think about the memories.

Don't think about the past.

He walked further down the street. He didn't feel as lousy as yesterday, at least. That was something. The pain wasn't as intense today. Still bad, sure, but nowhere near as strong. He felt like he'd found a happy medium.

He thought about how he'd been taken into hospital. How reluctant he was to have his hands seen to.

Because he knew Doctor Khaleed would know exactly what he was looking at.

He knew Doctor Khaleed would know damn well his wounds were self-inflicted.

And he didn't want anything like that being discovered or acknowledged.

He could barely look in the mirror and admit it to himself.

He took a deep breath of the warm air. A flashback to child-hood. A nicer flashback this time. A memory of being on a swing in a park. Mum pushing him as he got higher and higher. Laugh-ing. Both of them laughing. The sunlight twinkling against the duck pond in the distance. The sight of parents pushing prams. A feeling of happiness everywhere.

And then he flashed to the memory of getting home to Dad.

Of Dad asking Mum where they'd both been for the day.

The way he looked at Billy with something in his eyes.

Something that felt like... like hatred.

Something he just couldn't put his finger on at the time, but something he understood clearly now.

He gritted his teeth, which were already ground right down at the molars.

He kept on walking towards Jorah's place, the tension in his jaw hurting his ears now.

He went to take a right when he bumped into someone and almost lost his footing.

"Whoa," Billy said.

"Sorry. I wasn't..."

And then it clicked.

Both of them clicked.

Faye.

"Oh," Faye said, staring up at him with those glistening green eyes. "Billy. Hi."

Billy nodded at her. Cheeks flushing. Shit. Why did he always have to go and bump into Faye in the most uncomfortable circumstances imaginable? Then again, it couldn't be much worse than vomiting and collapsing, could it? It'd be a high bar to end up topping that on the embarrassment scale.

But, hey. This interaction wasn't over yet. There was time.

"Faye," he said, rubbing the back of his neck. "You're... you're up early."

"Oh," Faye said, batting her eyelashes and looking away. She was blushing too. "I... I like a morning run."

"You like a morning run?"

"Yeah. That's... that's kind of what I just said."

Shit. It was *exactly* what she'd just said. Be less fucking autistic, Billy. Do your absolute worst. "Yeah. Cool."

Great. Great effort. *Yeah. Cool.* Absolute Casanova over here.

"What you doing up and about, anyway?"

"Oh," Billy said. "I mean, I guess I like getting up early these days. Watching the sunrise. Little walk in the woods. That sort of thing."

Faye nodded. "And you're feeling better?"

"Oh. Yeah. Yeah, I'm fine. Think it was just the heat, you know?"

She looked down at him. "And your hands... They... They're better now?"

Billy looked down at his bandaged hands, and his stomach sank.

The bandages were red.

Blood trickled down the tip of his right index finger and dripped onto the hot tarmac pavement beneath him.

He tightened his grip, doing all he could to stop the bleeding. And then he forced something that resembled a smile. "Yeah. Hands... hands are getting better."

Faye smiled back at him. But she didn't look convinced.

"Anyway," she said.

"Yeah. Anyway."

"The run won't finish itself."

"No. Run won't finish..." Shit. What the hell was he even supposed to say?

In the end, he decided on saying nothing else. Just watched Faye walk past him, then start running off down the street, bronze legs glowing in the sunlight.

She glanced back around at him.

He turned away instantly. Didn't want her to think he was a creep.

He took a deep breath, swallowed a lump in his throat, and kept on walking towards Jorah's. What he had to do was simple. Just tell him he didn't want to take him up on his offer. Did he feel bad about it? Sure. Especially since Jorah was apparently on his last legs.

But at the end of the day, he couldn't let Jorah's predicament sway his own decision.

Rejecting the offer was the right thing to do.

He reached the front gate to Jorah's house and stopped right outside it.

His garden was overgrown and full of dandelions and weeds. People whispered behind his back about how much of a dump it looked, but Jorah insisted it was great for wildlife.

And watching the bees buzz around right now, Billy couldn't deny he probably had a point.

He took another deep breath and walked down the cracked pathway.

Just tell him the truth.

That's all he had to do.

Tell him the truth and get it done with.

Sorry, Jorah. I really appreciate your offer. But I don't think it's right. I don't think I'm the right man for the job. I don't think...

And then he noticed something.

Jorah's front door.

It wasn't properly shut.

It was ajar.

Billy stood there, and his heart thumped. He had no idea why he felt so nervous about this. Why he had such a bad feeling about it. But sometimes in life, you just know something is wrong. An intuition. A gut feeling.

This was one of those moments.

He lifted his fist. Went to knock on the door.

Waited for a response.

Nothing.

His mouth was dry. His head ached. He looked around, down the street, left and right.

Nobody in sight.

This wasn't right.

Something just didn't feel right.

"Jorah?" Billy said.

No response.

"Jorah!"

Again, silence.

Again, no response.

Billy knew what he should do. He should go report this immediately. Or just chill out. Because it was probably a mistake. He'd probably left his door open and nipped out. *Or* he'd left his door open and was still asleep. It was still early, after all. People made mistakes. Especially when they were seriously ill.

Right?

He felt torn between reporting this, between just leaving it, and another option, too.

Taking a look.

Taking a look for himself.

He gritted his teeth even harder.

The throbbing ache in his head growing stronger.

He took another deep, nervous breath.

And then he sighed.

Here goes nothing.

He pushed Jorah's front door open, and he stepped inside.

There was nobody in the lounge. Nobody sitting on that ornate leather sofa. A couple of wine glasses on the carpet, one of them with a drop of wine still sitting at the bottom.

He walked through the lounge towards the kitchen at the back. "Jorah? You okay?"

He popped his head around the kitchen.

No sign of Jorah.

He turned to the stairs and looked up.

He felt nervous. Really nervous. He didn't know *what* he would find. But something just screamed out at him that this was wrong.

This was very wrong.

Maybe he'd died.

Maybe he'd finally succumbed to the cancer after all.

And as far as Billy was aware... he was the only one who knew about it.

"Jorah?"

His voice echoed up the stairs into the silence above.

He didn't want to go up there. He wanted to turn around and walk back onto the street.

There was just this heavy feeling in the middle of his chest that he would discover something he really, really didn't want to discover.

But he walked up the stairs.

Step by creaking step.

He walked until he reached the top of the stairs, and then he stopped.

He saw Jorah's bedroom door right in front of him.

Ajar.

No sounds behind it.

None whatsoever.

"Jorah?" he called.

Nothing.

He looked back downstairs.

Wondered if there was still time to turn around.

Still time to get out of here.

But in the end, he knew he had no choice.

He walked across the carpet.

Walked over to Jorah's bedroom door.

He stopped in front of it.

Stood there.

Heart racing faster and faster.

He clenched his jaw.

Prayed this was a misunderstanding.

Prayed there was going to be an honest explanation for everything.

Prayed that he was just overthinking.

He took another deep breath, and then he pushed Jorah's bedroom door open.

When he saw what lay on the bed right in front of him, he knew his niggling sense that something was wrong had turned out right all along.

Only this was worse than he expected.

Far, far worse.

CHAPTER TEN

Jorah was dead. That much was clear.

And it wasn't exactly a shocking discovery in itself. Because Jorah had told Billy he was dying. He'd told him he was on his last legs. That he didn't have long to live. So being surprised at finding his body wasn't what rattled him.

What rattled Billy was Jorah's condition.

Because it was pretty fucking clear he hadn't died of natural causes.

Jorah lay slumped over on his side. The white bedsheets were covered in deep red blood. So much blood that it'd completely changed the colour of the sheets. A smell of metallic rust in the air, as well as shit.

The sound of flies buzzing around. Landing on Jorah's body, wandering around and exploring him, and then floating off again.

And the stab wounds.

The stab wounds all over Jorah's bare chest.

All over his torso.

So many stab marks that his punctured innards dangled out of his body.

Billy tasted vomit. He couldn't understand what he was looking at. Couldn't wrap his head around any of it.

Because Jorah.

Sure, some people weren't mad keen on him. Some people criticised some of his decisions and choices. Billy counted himself as one of those people. Never Jorah's biggest fan.

But *this*.

This was butchery.

This was the work of someone who hated Jorah. Who despised him.

He stepped further into Jorah's bedroom, over towards his body. His heart raced. He felt dizzy. Sick. He needed to report this. He needed to report it immediately.

Because there was absolutely no doubt about what this was.

This was murder.

Someone had murdered Jorah in the night.

And whoever had murdered him certainly didn't care that anyone would know it was murder. They hadn't tried to do this subtly. They hadn't tried to make it look accidental or like it could be natural.

Whoever had done this detested Jorah, and they'd made no effort to cover their feelings up.

He walked right over to Jorah's side. Looked down into his eyes, which stared blankly into nothingness. A glaze to them. Like a waxwork model.

"Jesus," Billy said, the taste of vomit growing stronger in his mouth as the shock of the scene hit him harder.

The contrast of that deep red blood against Jorah's pale skin.

Those deep gashes all over his body.

The flies buzzing around, oblivious to the horror of the scene.

And the smell.

Oh God, the *smell*.

He stood there, and he didn't know what to do. He didn't

know where he went from here. Where did *anyone* go from a discovery like this?

He just knew he couldn't stay here.

He had to report this.

He had to go to the Eastbrook police, and he had to report it.

He went to walk away from the bed when he heard something downstairs.

Footsteps.

He froze.

Footsteps.

Footsteps climbing the stairs.

Someone was here.

He wasn't alone.

He had visions of the killer.

Visions of the person who had done this to Jorah.

Visions of them creeping up on him.

Attacking him.

Butchering him, too.

And they wouldn't hesitate with him, that was for sure. Because far more people were ambivalent or didn't like Billy than Jorah—or so he thought, anyway.

So he had to be ready for whatever was coming up the stairs.

*Who*ever was coming up the stairs.

He tensed his fists and walked over to Jorah's bedroom door.

Opened it.

Stepped outside and braced himself for whoever was coming.

He had to be ready to defend himself.

He had to be ready to fight.

He had to be...

The garage.

The darkness.

The damp.

The cold hands against his body...

No. Not now. Not now...

He tried to push back against the memories as he stood there, frozen. His knees buckling. The anxiety taking over.

Climbing from his stomach, through his body, right up into his neck.

Making his heart beat faster.

Making breathing harder.

Not now, not now, not now...

He tried to remember the rules he'd heard.

The rules about accepting it.

The rules about just letting the fear be.

The rules about just trusting it would disappear on its own.

He thought about those rules as he listened to the footsteps creep further up the stairs, and then they stopped.

The footsteps stopped.

No more creaking.

No more sounds.

Nothing.

Billy stood there. Frozen. Couldn't move.

There was somebody here.

There was somebody here, and they were creeping towards him.

And whoever they were... Billy had an awful feeling it was the killer.

That they'd come back to remove some evidence.

Or worse.

He stood there, totally still. There were still no creaking noises. Still no more footsteps up the stairs. What were they doing?

He stood right there, and he waited.

But still, no sounds at all.

He kept on breathing through his nostrils, right into his stomach, as his arms tingled with anxiety and his chest tightened in front of his racing heart.

He stood there, and he knew he couldn't just wait here any longer.

He had to see who was climbing the stairs.

He had to see who was coming.

And he had to be ready to fight.

He took another breath.

Stepped forward.

When he saw what was on the stairs, Billy froze once again.

Because there was nothing on the stairs.

There was nobody on the stairs.

Nobody at all.

Jorah's house was empty, except for him.

Whoever was here, they had already gone.

CHAPTER ELEVEN

"So you're telling me you found him in this state?"

"That's exactly what I'm saying, yeah. And what I've been saying all along."

"You just walked in and found him like this?"

"Again. That's what I've been saying. Nothing's changed there."

"Just so happened to be wandering around in Jorah's house and found him dead?"

"Look," Billy said. "I know what you're getting at. And I know how it looks. I'm the one who found him. And I know that doesn't exactly make me look great here. But this is how I found him. And this is why I'm telling you. There's nothing more to it than that."

Sergeant Kirk sat opposite him with his arms wrapped around his large waist. He was far bigger than any man had any right to be in a world without power and a world where processed confectionary was no longer a thing.

He looked across this chipped table in this grim, grey-walled interview room at Billy. Billy could see the way he stared at him suspiciously. And he got it. Really, he did. Finding a body was never an enviable position to be in. Especially a body that had clearly been killed.

And the body of the leader of this entire community?

Yeah. Yeah, that was something else entirely.

Kirk sat in silence. Stared at Billy. It was as if he was trying to break him by staring at him. But really, it just made him look like he was a bit simple. If this was his way of trying to coax Billy into admitting something or figuring out whether he was guilty, then he wasn't doing a very good job, quite frankly.

"I just... I just can't wrap my head around it," Kirk said.

"Me neither."

"Jorah. He was a pompous bastard at times. But he... he was a good man. A good leader. I don't know why anyone would do this to him. To put him through that suffering. I just don't get it."

"He was sick," Billy said.

"What?"

"He was sick. Late-stage cancer, apparently. Told me yesterday when I was in the hospital. And he also told me..."

He stopped, then. The memory. The memory of what Jorah told him. Of what he proposed to him.

The offer to take up the leadership reins at Eastbrook.

An offer Billy felt like he truly couldn't accept.

An offer that had surely died with Jorah.

"Told you what?" Kirk asked.

"Nothing," Billy said. "I just... I guess I was worried about him. After what he told me. So I went to see him. The door was ajar. I just had a bad feeling. And when I found him..."

The deep gashes across his chest.

Piercing his hairy belly.

The dead look in his frozen eyes.

"Do you remember seeing anything else suspicious? Anyone lurking around his place or anything like that?"

Billy shook his head. "It's just like I said. Nobody around. Swore I heard someone in there, though. Someone creeping around. But by the time I got to the top of the stairs, they were already gone."

Kirk sighed again. He liked sighing a lot, this guy. If there was one reaction quite clearly his favourite, it was certainly a sigh. "I don't even know where to begin with this news. How to break it. With the tape up, I'm sure word's already travelling. But when it's made official... God, this is gonna break Eastbrook."

Billy nodded. He didn't know what to say. Kirk was probably right. Eastbrook had suffered tragedy before, but Jorah was always a constant. What happened next, Billy had no idea.

But whatever happened next, the question of Jorah's death would surely loom large over this community like a ghost.

And the people here wouldn't settle until it was resolved.

"I'll have to conduct a formal investigation," Kirk said, sighing again. "And in the meantime... it was always protocol that the council would take over Eastbrook before electing a new leader. I'm a member of that council. So I'll inform the others, and we can get things in gear."

The council. Jeez, what a smug bunch of bastards. A way of Jorah making it seem like decisions didn't just come through him, a way of preventing a dictatorship. The council always had to approve decisions about Eastbrook unanimously—from lofty decisions about end-of-life care to pointless minutiae like whether to paint a house white or off-white. Whatever the decision, the council always had a say.

And the worst thing about the council?

The fact that Marco, one of the smuggest bastards ever to have lived, sat on it.

Billy pictured the fake crying and the smug self-satisfaction of the council when they found out about Jorah's death. And he knew deep down, they'd all be happy that they had total control, even if it was just for a short period.

He thought about Jorah's offer. Telling him about his sickness.

And then the offer of a leadership role. And just how much a decision like that would piss the council off.

"Are you absolutely sure everything you are telling me is accurate?" Kirk asked. "Because if there's anything we're missing... anything at all that might assist. It could be helpful."

Billy heard how Kirk said those words, and he knew what he was getting at.

It could be helpful.

Helpful to him more than anyone.

He thought about the leadership offer. Opened his mouth to tell Kirk everything.

And then he closed it, and he shook his head.

Kirk sighed—again. He jotted a few things down on a notepad, which Billy was convinced was covered in scribbles. "Okay. Well. You're free to go."

"Really?"

"Sure. Why?"

"I just thought—"

"Is there a reason I wouldn't let you go?"

Reverse psychology bullshit. That stupid stare, once again.

The bastard thought he was cleverer than he actually was.

"No," Billy said. "I just... It's like you said. I know how it is."

Kirk nodded. But he didn't look convinced.

Billy stood up. Walked over towards the door. He couldn't wait to get out of this sauna of a room. He was sweaty, he was hot, and he was tired.

And he could feel anxiety creeping up inside him.

Clawing its way from his stomach to his chest.

"Oh, Billy?" Kirk asked.

Billy stopped. Turned around. "Huh?"

"Your hands," Kirk said. "Sure everything's okay with them?"

Billy looked down and saw blood trickling from his right hand onto the interview room's dirty white floor.

Tightened his fists again to stop the flow.

"I ... Yeah," Billy said. "Yeah. They're fine."

But Kirk studied him closely.

He didn't look convinced.

"Don't go far," he said.

"What?"

"You know exactly what I said. And what I mean."

Billy looked into his eyes and noticed they didn't seem as empty anymore.

They seemed more menacing.

More threatening.

Billy took a deep breath, and he nodded. "Understood."

He walked out of the interview room and out into the old police station.

Blood trickled down from the interview room handle and onto the dirty floor.

CHAPTER TWELVE

"I mean, it's not exactly a great look, is it, Billy?"

Billy closed his eyes and sighed. Shit. He must be catching the sighing bug from Sergeant Kirk. As long as he didn't catch the waistline to go with it, and the premature ageing, too. Really didn't fancy looking in his forties while he was still only mid-twenties. A whole lifetime in this powerless world ahead of him, after all.

He sat in Steve's lounge and rubbed his hands against his burning eyes. It was frigging roasting in here. Steve always insisted on having all the windows shut because he was afraid of wasps. Seriously, wasps. He'd been through fifteen years of no power, spent tons of years living alone in a sewer, and was afraid of *frigging* wasps.

"I know it's not a great look," Billy said. "I wish people would stop telling me it's not a great look. I get that part. But what the hell was I supposed to do? Not go inside? Not investigate? Not report it?"

Steve sighed—oh great. Now *he* had the sighing bug, too. "I know it ain't ideal. I just... God, I wish it was anyone but you who'd found him."

"Tell me about it," Billy said.

They sat there in silence. Billy's heart wouldn't stop racing. Only three months had passed since the incident with Jarrod and the Animals, and it felt like he hadn't been grateful enough for the peace. Especially since the years before had been so peaceful, too.

Because this... the murder of the leader...

This was going to change things.

"You know what people are going to say, don't you?"

Billy puffed out his lips and shook his head. "They can say whatever the hell they want to say."

"I mean, it don't look great—"

"There it is, again. I know. I know it doesn't look great. But what the hell am I supposed to do?"

Steve nodded. Thankfully he didn't bloody sigh this time. "Sorry. I'm just... I guess you've been through enough lately. Don't want you getting burdened with even more crap."

"That's nice of you," Billy said.

"Don't be sarcastic."

"I'm not being sarcastic. I just... I don't get it. Jorah. First, this weird offer of leadership to me. Then Jorah winds up dead. And I'm the one to find him. I dunno. It all just seems a little..."

"Coincidental?" Steve said.

"What're you getting at?"

Steve shuffled forward in his chair. "Hear me out. But... but what if there's a link to all this crap?"

"A link?"

"What if... what if someone ain't happy about Jorah's plan to make you leader? What if they're unhappy enough about it that they'd go as far as killing him to stop you taking over?"

Billy shook his head. "I can't think of anyone that'd do anything like that here."

"People have sides to them they don't like to show. Real dirty sides. Don't be naive, kid. You know that just as well as I do."

Billy figured Steve had a point. He didn't like admitting it, but he did.

"Someone hears Jorah has plans for you to take over," Steve said. "They don't like it. So they take him out. Make it look like a murder. A real nasty murder. Plan to start a panic. Council seize control with their dirty hands. I dunno. It just... Something doesn't ring true for me, Billy."

"I'm not sure I like it when you speak like this."

"Look," Steve said. "You've told your truth. The best thing you can do is keep your head down. Stay out of the way while this investigation goes on. You've told the truth. You're innocent. And you ain't held anything back from Kirk. Right?"

Billy didn't say a word.

"Oh," Steve said. "So you *have* kept summat back from him?"

"I didn't tell him about Jorah's offer."

"Why didn't you tell him about that?"

"I don't know. I just... I guess I didn't see the relevance."

Steve tutted. "I mean, I guess it doesn't matter. Not really. But if Kirk knew what Jorah saw in you, it might've helped your case. But then... it might've put the spotlight even more on you. Made it look like you were just desperate to be leader. So desperate you'd—"

"Kill," Billy said.

Steve nodded.

Billy sat there and stared at Steve. Steve stared back at him. He couldn't believe he was actually having this conversation. It didn't feel real. It didn't feel right.

And as much as he was certain of his innocence... it felt like a dark cloud was looming overhead.

Ready to burst everywhere.

"The people are gonna know soon," Steve said. "And when they do... it ain't gonna be pretty. You know that. Like, you realise exactly what that means. Right?"

Billy swallowed a lump in his dry throat. He nodded. "I can take a bit of judgement."

"This isn't gonna just be judgement, Billy. You've got to accept that in the eyes of a lot of people, the fact you were sniffing around there is gonna make you look guilty as hell. And that's what people are gonna believe. Because people would rather believe the wrong man's guilty than accept the truth."

"And what's the truth?" Billy asked.

Steve looked at his torn, brown curtains. The sunlight, desperately trying to burst its way through.

"The truth is... there's someone out there. Someone dangerous. Someone really bloody dangerous. We don't know what they want. We don't know what their motive is. But we know one thing for sure."

"And what's that?"

Steve took a breath. Looked Billy right in the eye. "Someone who's capable of doing what they did to Jorah is capable of anything."

Billy felt a shiver creep up his spine.

He needed to get out of here.

He stood up. "I should probably—"

He didn't finish his sentence.

Because something smashed through the window.

Landed right in the middle of Steve's lounge, tearing through the curtains.

"Holy hell," Steve said, jumping from his chair, peering outside. "What the hell?"

But Billy didn't see what was outside.

He just saw the brick.

The red writing smeared across it.

KILLER.

CHAPTER THIRTEEN

Billy sat awake in bed, and every sound he heard, he was convinced it was someone coming to bump him off too.

The brick through Steve's window had shaken him up. He knew people would jump to conclusions about him being the killer. He was at the scene of the crime, after all. He was the one to find Jorah's body. A few side-glances and a bit of uncertainty around him were only going to be natural for a time.

But that brick through the window.

That word smeared onto it in blood.

KILLER.

Whoever did that had targeted him. And to do that—to throw a brick through Steve's window—was a strong, aggressive move.

It reminded Billy just how under the spotlight he was.

And it made him realise just how in danger he was.

He listened to the storm outside. Thunder exploding above. Every now and then, lightning flashed, filling the room with light, like someone was outside taking a photograph. It felt like that, in a way. Felt like his every move was under scrutiny. Felt like he was being watched.

He couldn't sleep. Sleep was a write-off at this stage. Exhausted, but wired as fuck. His only option was to sit up against the wall and stare across the room into the darkness. Listening to the thunder. Listening to the rain.

But as much as he tried to zone out, all he could think about was Jorah.

He thought about the sight of his body lying on its side in a heap.

He thought about the large stab wounds on his torso, his chest, his neck, even his face.

A savage attack. Whoever had committed that attack really didn't like Jorah. Which, again, just puzzled Billy.

But there was that other option too.

The possibility that Steve had raised.

What if someone *had* heard Jorah's conversation with Billy?

What if this really *was* someone determined for Billy not to follow in Jorah's footsteps?

But then... the savagery. The brutality with which the crime had been committed.

It just didn't add up.

He stood up. Walked across his bedroom floor, being careful not to wake Rex—although, not too much to worry about there, because waking Rex was a gargantuan task in itself nowadays.

He walked over to his bedroom window. Looked outside. Out at the pouring rain. Out at the terraced houses. Out at the street outside.

Empty.

Not a soul in sight.

Which wasn't unusual, per se. It was late, after all.

But everyone was in early tonight.

Nobody wanted to take any chances.

Not after what happened to Jorah.

Although...

That happened in the comfort of his own home.

Which meant nowhere was safe.

He stood at the window, looked out into the darkness, and he knew the next few days and weeks weren't going to be easy. Jorah's memorial. The investigation into his death. The election of a new leader.

It was going to be a time of great upheaval for the entire community. And it wasn't going to be an easy process to go through.

He went to go back to bed when he saw something.

Something that made him freeze.

Somebody was out there.

Out there on the opposite side of the road.

Staring up into his bedroom window.

He blinked a few times. Wondered if he was just imagining things. Because what kind of lunatic would be out here in this torrential rain? This storm?

But they didn't disappear when he blinked.

They weren't a hallucinatory product of his stressed, exhausted imagination.

They were right here.

He looked down at that figure, standing there in the darkness. It creeped him out, seeing them looking up towards him. His first thought was that it must be the unknown assailant who'd thrown the brick through Steve's window.

But then he wondered if this could be even deeper than his first suspicion.

What if they were here to kill him?

What if Steve's conspiracy theory was true?

He went to take a step back into his room. He had no choice. He had to wrap up. He had to go outside. He had to confront whoever it was and see what the hell they wanted. What the hell they were doing outside his home in the middle of the night, staring up into his window.

What the hell was going on.

He took a step back towards his bed when suddenly, he heard something that made his skin turn cold.

Downstairs, he heard footsteps.

CHAPTER FOURTEEN

Billy heard the footsteps downstairs and, not gonna lie, he shat himself a little bit.

Metaphorically, of course.

Maybe.

Hopefully.

He stood in the middle of his bedroom and stared at the window. Lightning flashed, filling the darkness with light, just for a split second.

And as he stood there, listening to the rain hammering down on the roof, he felt the hairs on his arms stand right on end.

Somebody was downstairs.

Somebody was in his house.

He turned around to the bedroom door. Rex lay beside it. He hadn't budged an inch. Not as sharp as he used to be. Nowhere near.

And as Billy stood there, a plethora of possibilities spiralled around his mind. All of them equally terrifying.

Someone was here to fuck with him.

Someone was here to kick the shit out of him.

Someone was here to kill him.

He took a deep, shaky breath in. Strained to hear any more movement downstairs. Maybe it was just Steve. Maybe he'd just come in to check on him and make sure he was okay.

But no.

That didn't make any sense.

Steve wouldn't do that to him. He wouldn't scare him like that. Not at the moment, with everything going on.

There was no doubt in Billy's mind that whoever was in his house right now had something to do with Jorah's death.

He swallowed a lump, his mouth dry. Looked back around at the window. And he thought back to that figure.

The figure he'd seen standing outside.

Staring up at him.

What did they have to do with all this?

It had to be linked. It had to be related.

It couldn't be coincidence.

Maybe they were watching to make sure whatever *whoever* had planned for Billy went down without issue.

He thought back to Jorah's.

To those footsteps coming up the stairs.

Climbing the stairs, then... gone.

What if they weren't in his imagination, as he was beginning to believe?

What if they were real?

And what if they were the same people downstairs in his house right now?

He walked over to the window. Lifting his feet felt like walking through tar.

He reached the window.

Looked outside.

Across the road, in the falling rain, there was nobody there anymore.

They were gone.

He looked out there. Heart racing faster. Mouth growing drier.

And then he heard it again.

Another creak downstairs.

Footsteps.

He turned around and walked across the bedroom, over to the door. Opened it with his shaking hand and peeked out into the darkness of his landing. If he thought too hard about shit before doing it, he'd seize up. Wouldn't be able to move a muscle.

He had to go down there.

He had to find out whoever this was.

He could defend himself. He could win a fight. He could...

His hands.

The pain right in the middle of his shaking palms.

Okay. Maybe he wasn't as capable as he used to be. Maybe he wasn't as strong as he used to be.

But he'd still back himself to win a fight.

He looked over to the corner of his room. The heavy baseball bat propped up against the wall.

Walked over to it.

Grabbed it.

He needed to be ready for whatever he was about to face.

He stepped out onto the landing. Walked over to the top of the stairs. Another bolt of lightning flashed, filling the landing with light.

He heard another creaking noise downstairs. Or was that upstairs with him? Was it in the loft? He wasn't sure. Every single sound was magnified. Every single noise put him on edge.

He needed to keep his shit together.

Get the hell downstairs.

Figure out who the hell was in his house.

And then...

Well. He didn't need to think about what happened next. Not yet.

He began to walk down the stairs. Heart pounding. Chest tight. He felt like he was descending into Hell itself. He figured he was, in a way.

Because he wasn't going to find anything good, that was for sure.

He kept on descending the stairs. Thunder roared above. Lightning flashed more frequently. The rain fell heavier, hammering against the roof.

He got to the bottom of the stairs, and he stopped.

His lounge door was closed. Which suggested nobody was in there.

But the kitchen door...

He usually closed it. But he couldn't remember if he had or not.

But it was open now.

It was open now, which made him wonder.

Was someone in there?

He swallowed another lump in his throat.

Gripped his baseball bat tighter.

And he walked down the corridor, right towards the kitchen door.

Step, by step, by step.

He reached the kitchen door. Heart racing. Aching hands gripping shakily onto the baseball bat.

He peered into the darkness.

He didn't see any movement in there.

Anyone hiding in the shadows.

But that didn't mean they weren't.

They could be watching.

They could be waiting.

Waiting for the perfect moment...

He stood at the door, his heart beating faster and faster, and suddenly something caught his eye.

On the table.

Something he hadn't seen before.

Something *he* definitely hadn't put there.

He couldn't make it out. Not properly. Not in the darkness.

But when the lightning flashed, he saw exactly what it was, and his entire body went cold.

There could be no doubt anymore.

Someone was fucking with him.

CHAPTER FIFTEEN

Okay. So one thing was for sure.

Billy had *definitely* not left a bloody knife lying in the middle of his kitchen table before he went to bed.

But there it was. Sitting there, right in the middle of his kitchen table. Staring up at him, glowing in the moonlight, which shone down on it like stage lighting.

A knife.

A knife covered in blood.

On his kitchen table.

In his home.

His skin turned cold. He felt sick. His knees were weak. His head was spinning in circles.

This couldn't be real.

This had to be a nightmare.

And yet...

He walked over to that knife. Stood over it. He knew he was barking up the wrong tree, but he figured if he got closer to it, he might realise he was seeing things. That he'd got it wrong. He was just tired. Exhausted. Or it was something else entirely. Not a knife. Not a knife covered in blood.

But the closer he got to it, the more his suspicions were confirmed.

It was a knife. No fucking doubt about it.

And looking at the blood, looking at the little chunks of flesh clinging to it, there was no doubt in Billy's mind that this was the weapon used to kill Jorah.

Here in his kitchen.

Here in his home.

He stood there. Totally still. He didn't know what the fuck to do. What *could* he do? How could he possibly explain this? If he told Kirk about it, then it was over for him. He was finished. If he told *anyone* about it, it could be dangerous. It could get back to him.

No. As much as he knew he was putting himself in deep shit by not telling the truth, there was absolutely no doubt in Billy's mind that he needed to get rid of this knife.

Because someone had planted it here.

Someone was trying to set him up.

This went beyond simply taking Jorah out in a power grab.

This was a set up.

And Billy was right in the frame.

He heard rustling over his shoulder.

Turned around.

Nobody there.

Nothing but an empty hallway.

Nothing but darkness.

He turned back to the kitchen table. Hoped to God the knife would be gone. That it was all in his head. That he was imagining this entire shitty situation.

But his prayers weren't answered.

Of course they fucking weren't.

The knife was still there.

Covered in blood.

He swallowed a lump in his throat. Fuck. He couldn't tell anyone about this. And he couldn't leave the knife here, either.

He had to get it out of this house.

He didn't want to touch it. He didn't want to incriminate himself in any way.

But fuck. He would have to touch it if he wanted to get it out of here.

He grabbed a towel from the side and picked it up.

Wrapped it around the knife and stuffed it under his shirt.

And without thinking any more about it, he walked to his front door.

Opened it.

Looked back around, back into the darkness.

He couldn't put his finger on it. But he couldn't shake the feeling there was still somebody in there.

Watching his every move.

He turned around, and he walked out of his home. Walked down the dark, empty road. Rain hammered down from above, drenching him. He felt like the eyes of the community were on him. Like people were in their windows staring down at him. Watching him and wondering what he was doing.

He just had to get to the fence.

He had to get to the fence, and he had to get to the woods, and he had to get the knife the hell away from—

Footsteps.

Footsteps behind him.

He spun around.

Nobody there.

No movement in sight.

He swallowed a lump in his throat and turned around again. Kept his head down and started walking. Just a walk. Just a walk in the middle of the night. Nothing suspicious about it. Nothing suspicious at all.

No. Sure. You're the prime suspect in this murder and you're wandering through the street in the middle of the night. I'm sure that's a really bloody good look...

He saw the gates up ahead. Saw a couple of guards on watch. Fuck. He couldn't go that way. Definitely didn't want to have to explain himself right now.

And definitely didn't want to risk being searched.

He looked at the houses to his left. At the trees behind them. He'd have to go over that way. Hide the knife somewhere. Wait until tomorrow before taking it as far away from Eastbrook as possible. At least it would be out of his hands. Away from his property.

He went to head over to those houses when suddenly he heard something that made him freeze.

Footsteps.

Walking towards him.

He stood still.

Stood totally still as those footsteps got closer.

They were coming for him.

They were coming for him, and they were going to find him carrying the knife, and it would be over.

It would be completely over.

He turned around.

Bracing himself for whoever the hell was out here on his tail at this time.

When he saw who it was, the hairs on the back of his neck stood right on end.

A figure.

A figure standing there in the darkness.

Staring right at him.

He couldn't see their face. But they were watching him.

Watching him closely.

It was the person from before.

The one he'd seen outside his window.

"What do you want?" Billy said.

The figure didn't respond.

Just stood there, totally still.

Staring.

That was it. He wasn't standing around being haunted by this creep any longer. It was time to confront him. Properly. Figure out who the hell it was screwing with him.

Because this was serious.

And if Billy didn't get to the bottom of it, he would find himself in deeper shit than he was already in.

He went to walk towards the figure when suddenly, the figure ran off towards the right.

Billy ran after him. He wasn't playing games anymore. Whoever it was, they weren't going to fuck with him again.

But when Billy reached the turn in the road the figure disappeared around, he didn't see anybody.

The street was empty.

The figure was gone.

Like they'd vanished into thin air.

He stared down the street. Moonlight shone down from above. Heavy rain waterfalled down the street. His heart thumped against his chest. And in his hands, underneath his shirt, he felt the knife burning against his skin like poison.

He didn't get it. None of it made sense. Who was out to get him? Why were they fucking with him like this?

And where the hell had they gone?

He stood there, looked down the street, and he sighed.

Whatever the case, they weren't here anymore.

They were gone now.

But they'll be back.

The thought made him shiver.

Whatever the case, the situation was still the same. He had the knife. The murder weapon. And he had to get rid of it. Fast.

He went to turn around when suddenly, out of nowhere, he heard a voice.

"Hello, Billy. Someone's up late."

He froze.

Fuck. Please don't be who I think it is. Please, please *don't be who I think it is...*

But when Billy turned around, he saw it was exactly who he fucking thought it was.

"Alright, Billy?" Marco said.

CHAPTER SIXTEEN

Marco was definitely the last fucking person on Earth Billy wanted to run into while holding on to the murder weapon that most probably killed Jorah, that was for sure.

But fuck. The way the last few days were going, he should've expected another frigging spanner in the works, shouldn't he?

Marco stood there, soaked in rain. Stared at Billy. It was weird, for one. Why the hell was Marco out here in the first place? It was the middle of the night. What was he doing here?

Why was he watching Billy?

And could he have something to do with all this weirdness?

"Strange night to be out for a walk," Marco said.

"I could say the same about you."

Marco smiled. "I only came out because I saw you lurking around out here. Didn't realise it was you at first. Thought someone was snooping about. And after what happened to Jorah... well."

Shit. What could Billy even say? What argument did he possibly have for being out here in the middle of the night—the night after Jorah had been murdered?

Holding the frigging *murder weapon,* no less?

Damn it. He really hadn't thought this through. And now he *was* thinking it through, he realised what an absolutely shitty and terrible idea it was all along.

"I thought I saw someone too," Billy said. Shuffling the knife around in his hands, under his shirt.

"Oh yeah?"

"Yeah. And... and I did. Actually. I thought I heard someone snooping around my place. Went downstairs and... Well. I saw someone looking through my window. And again just now. You know anything about that?"

"I'm not the one wandering through the street in the middle of the night," Marco said.

"Well. You kind of are. Technically."

"I don't know what your deal is," Marco said, walking towards Billy, a sudden shift to his demeanour and tone from the calm and collected to... to anger. "Making jokes like that. Right after Jorah's death. Some would say you look pretty guilty."

"Yeah," Billy said. "So much so Steve got a brick through the window for it. Would you know anything about that?"

Marco shook his head. "You can't blame people for feeling suspicious. And right now, you aren't exactly helping your case."

Billy looked into Marco's eyes, and he wondered. Could it be as he theorised? Had someone bumped Jorah off because they'd heard Billy was going to take over as leader?

Or was there more to it than that?

The knife on the table.

Was this about Billy? Pinning something on him?

Or could it be both?

Could it be...

"You were there in the hospital," Billy said.

Marco narrowed his eyes. "What's that got to do with anything?"

"When you found me yesterday. You were at the hospital.

Jorah... Jorah came in and spoke to me. And you were there. Weren't you?"

"I don't see what this has to do with anything."

"You heard us. Talking about... You heard, and you just couldn't bear it, could you?"

"I really don't follow, Billy. But now you mention it, yeah. I was there. And seeing how unstable you've been lately, I'm beginning to wonder."

"What?"

"Well. Your hands. Your mental state. That whole fucking buffet of problems you've got. I'm starting to wonder if Jorah said something to you. Fired you. And that you just couldn't bear the thought of it."

"You bastard," Billy said. "You absolute bastard."

"Hey," Marco said, raising his hands. "What're you gonna do? Kill me too?"

"I had nothing to do with Jorah's death. And for what it's worth, he offered me a chance to take over. A chance to be leader. Which makes me wonder. Maybe *you* heard that. And being on that council of yours, maybe you saw an opportunity. A chance. And maybe you just couldn't bear the thought of me leading this place. So you did what you could. You killed him. And then you tried to frame me."

Marco just stood there as rain poured down from above. Stared. Didn't say a word.

And it frustrated Billy because he wanted him to bite back.

He wanted him to react.

He wanted him to give him *something*.

But Marco didn't say a word.

"It's what you've wanted ever since the attack on your people, isn't it?" Billy said. "Me, out of the way. Jorah out of the way. A chance to do things differently. It makes sense. It makes total sense. I just... I really didn't think you were that ruthless."

Still, Marco stood there in the rain.

Still, he said nothing.

Just stood there and stared at Billy.

Like he was waiting for him to finish.

Neither of them speaking now.

Just the sound of the rain.

The sound of thunder rumbling overhead.

"So go on," Billy said. "Say something. Say whatever you've got to say. But I'm serious, Marco. I'm fucking serious. I will not go down for a crime I haven't committed."

Marco stayed silent a little while longer.

But this time, there was an end to the silence.

"Billy," he said. "Don't take this the wrong way. Please don't. But I'm starting to get a little worried about you."

Worried about him? What the hell was he—

"Passing out yesterday. All this nonsense about Jorah offering you a leadership role. And now this. Out here in the night making... making bizarre allegations."

"Bizarre allegations? Is that what we're calling them?"

"I know you've got some shit in your past. Some demons in your closet. Don't you think it's about time you properly faced them?"

That one hurt.

He felt that one like a punch to the gut.

Because those words, coming from Marco...

What did Marco know about his past?

His past.

Oh God, his past.

The garage.

The cold fingers against his skin.

The smelly, boozy lips against his face—

NO!

"I'm going home," Billy said, lowering his head, tightening his grip around the knife. Hands shaking. Just needed to be alone right now. Couldn't be here anymore.

"What are you hiding under your shirt, Billy?" Marco asked.

Billy stopped.

Stopped dead, right in the middle of the street.

Looked around at Marco.

"Don't act dumb," Marco said. "I've seen you twiddling your fingers under there for the last five minutes. Longer, in fact. What are you hiding?"

You know. You know exactly what it is, you stupid bastard, because you planted it.

But he couldn't say that.

He couldn't say it because he couldn't tell Marco what it was.

He couldn't—

"People think you did this," Marco said, walking towards him slowly. "People think you're the killer. They think you're nutty. That the shit that happened to you with those wolf people fucked you up. Not to mention... well. Let's just say I know a thing or two about some of your little secrets."

Billy's heart raced.

Marco stood there opposite, smirking.

Billy held on to the knife.

He wanted to drop it.

He wanted to let go.

But he couldn't.

He was trapped.

He was completely trapped.

Marco stood right opposite him now. So close Billy could smell the cheap aftershave on his sodden shirt. The smoke on his breath.

And he could see that smirk tugging at the corners of his mouth.

"I know what happened to you."

"Back off, Marco."

"I know what you went through."

"I said—"

"I know what Ramiro and his people did to you."

Ramiro.

It was that one word that did it.

That one word.

It swallowed Billy up.

It took him to that garage again.

It brought back the pain—

The slaps.

The punches.

The splitting agony and the taste of...

The next thing he knew, he was back here again.

He was back on the street again.

Only there was a problem.

He'd pulled out the knife.

And he had it pointed right at Marco.

Marco stood opposite him.

Stared at the knife with his wide eyes.

Then looked back at Billy.

And as the pair of them stood there in the torrential storm, none of them talking for what felt like forever, it was Marco who finally broke the silence.

"It *was* you."

CHAPTER SEVENTEEN

Billy stood there with the knife in hand, and he knew he'd messed up big time.

Marco stood opposite him. His eyes were wide. He stared right down at the knife in Billy's hand. If Billy could rewind time right now, he would. He'd keep the blade hidden. Or, fuck— he wouldn't have even come out here in the middle of the night at all.

But he couldn't rewind time. Nobody had that luxury.

He was here. And Marco was onto him.

And he was in deep, deep shit.

Marco stood there in the middle of this dark, empty street as rain lashed out from above. The moon shone down on both of them like a spotlight.

"It's not... it's not what it looks like," Billy said.

Marco looked up at him. Right into his eyes, now. And for a man Billy was convinced must be framing him... he looked genuinely shocked. Legitimately surprised by this knife.

It didn't make sense.

None of it made sense.

"You did it," Marco muttered. Quietly. "You... you killed Jorah."

Billy shook his head. He put the knife away, stuck it into his back pocket. "Marco, I didn't—"

"Don't move a muscle," Marco shouted.

"Marco—"

"Don't you dare move another muscle, Billy."

Marco had his hand raised. But his hand was shaking. He wasn't holding a weapon. Wasn't holding anything.

He looked afraid.

Afraid of Billy.

"You need to listen to me, Billy," Marco said. "You need... you need to come with me. Right now. Because—because you know it's the right thing to do. It's over. Whatever you've got going on... it's over. It can't go on any longer."

"I found this knife on my kitchen table," Billy said. "I thought... I started to think you'd planted it there."

"Me? Why the hell would I plant it there?"

"Because of the leadership thing. With Jorah. Because... because you hate me. To punish me. I don't know."

Marco shook his head. The way he looked at Billy told Billy everything he needed to know.

He thought Billy was crazy.

He thought Billy was unhinged.

And to be honest?

Billy hadn't exactly done the best job of proving otherwise, had he?

"I think... I think you need help, Billy."

"Don't patronise me with that bullshit."

"Don't patronise *you* with bullshit? You're the one threatening me with a bloody knife."

"I'm not... I'm not threatening you."

"You're the one going off about some—some conspiracy

against you. You know how you sound right now? Do you have any idea?"

"You were goading me," Billy said. "About my past. About shit you shouldn't even know about. How the hell was I supposed to react?"

"I wasn't *goading* you," Marco said. "I was..."

He stopped, then. Shook his head. "It doesn't matter. What matters is... is you need to come with me. You need to do the right thing. For yourself and everyone here. It's over, Billy. It's over."

Billy stood there in the darkness and the rain, and although he'd felt truly screwed a bunch of times in his life before, he wasn't sure he'd ever felt quite *this* screwed.

He felt the knife in his hand. He should never have picked it up. He should never have come out here carrying it. He should have stayed at home, and he should have reported it instead of making himself look more fucking guilty.

"Hand me the knife," Marco said. "Hand it over, and come with me. Don't do anything else you might regret."

And as much as Billy wanted to protest his innocence... he knew it was pointless. Completely and utterly pointless.

Marco had already made up his mind.

And could Billy argue with him? Really?

What would he think if the boot were on the other foot?

"How do you know about my past?" Billy said. "Why would— why would you say those things? And why were you following me?"

Marco just stood there, shaking his head. He was doing a very convincing job of looking shocked and innocent suddenly, Billy had to admit.

"It's like I said. I followed you because I saw you wandering the streets. Which is weird after what happened to Jorah today."

"My past. What do you know about my past? Why would— why would you provoke me like that?"

"I wasn't trying to provoke you."

"Bullshit. You goaded me. You—you goaded me, and you forced me to pull the knife and—"

"I wasn't trying to fucking provoke you," Marco said. "I was... I was there, Billy. I was there too."

A flashback.

The darkness of the garage.

The sound of whimpering and screaming.

Of skin slapping against skin.

The taste of vomit at the back of his throat.

And the glimpse of others.

Others, just like him.

Marco.

"You were... you were there," Billy said.

Marco stood opposite him in the rain. And suddenly, it clicked into place. Suddenly, it all made sense.

A deep, horrifying sense that Billy wanted to run from.

But sense all the same.

"You weren't the only kid who suffered at the hands of Ramiro's gang," Marco said. "But just be grateful you didn't end up with Jarrod."

Billy felt sick and dizzy. This was a nightmare. This couldn't be real.

Marco.

All these years, and he had no idea. No fucking clue.

"I know how it fucks with your head," Marco said. "I know the nightmares. I know the demons. But this... this is too far, Billy. This is way too far. You've gone over the edge. And it needs —it needs to stop. Right now."

And Billy couldn't say anything.

He couldn't think.

He could only look into Marco's eyes in the pouring rain and feel total, utter shame.

"I'm sorry," Billy said.

Marco shook his head. Billy couldn't tell whether he was crying or whether it was just rain. "It's not too late to make the right decision. Come on. Let's... let's get you to the station. Let's end this."

But as Billy stood there in the rain, he knew he couldn't go with Marco.

Because he hadn't done this.

He hadn't killed Jorah.

He knew how it looked. But he hadn't committed this crime.

He looked down the street. Down towards where that mystery figure disappeared. He had no idea who it was. He knew Marco and everyone else here would just claim he was insane.

But he knew he was right.

"I didn't kill him," Billy said. "And that's why I've got to do what I'm going to do. Hopefully, you'll understand, one day."

Marco narrowed his eyes. "What..."

But Billy didn't wait for him to finish.

He turned around and ran into the night.

CHAPTER EIGHTEEN

Billy didn't stop running.

He ran through the trees. He had no idea where he was, only that he was deep into the woods. Deeper than he'd ever been. It was pitch black in here. The trees suffocated the moonlight. Rain fell heavily from above. Every now and then, he heard the rumble of thunder.

But he just kept on running.

Even though he was completely drenched.

Even though a crippling stitch attacked his stomach.

And even though he knew exactly how this made him look.

Guilty.

He couldn't stop running because he knew Marco would have alerted the guards. There would be people running after him, chasing him, trying to stop him. And again, as he'd said before, he couldn't exactly blame them. He was the one who found Jorah's body. He was the one carrying the murder weapon and threatening Marco in the street with it in the middle of the night.

He couldn't blame anyone for holding him responsible.

But he hadn't killed Jorah. And he wasn't going to go down for doing something he hadn't done.

Even if that meant running away.

But as he ran, as his legs grew weaker and the soles of his feet more sore, he began to realise he was running away from far more than just the prospect of incarceration.

Marco.

The things he'd told him about his own past.

How he'd been through what Billy had been through, too...

The knowledge that somebody else like him had been living alongside him all along...

Billy shook his head and forced that thought from his mind. But then more thoughts crept up on him, invaded his consciousness.

Was that what it all boiled down to?

Did Marco detest him because he hadn't had it "as rough" because he'd never ended up with Jarrod?

No. He had no idea. He had no fucking clue whatsoever.

He just knew that he needed to keep running.

He needed to get as far from Eastbrook as he possibly could.

Because he wasn't being made to suffer for something he hadn't done.

As he ran past more trees, deeper and deeper into these woods, he thought about Rex. Alone at home. And Steve, too. Steve and Faye were going to find out about Marco's confrontation with him in the street in the middle of the night.

And he hated that he wouldn't be there to give his side.

He hated how disappointed Steve would be in him. And Faye, too. How shocked she'd be to hear Marco's version of events.

He wanted to do something about it. He wanted to tell his side of the story.

But nobody would believe him anyway.

And going back to Eastbrook now, after doing a runner?

That was suicide.

Total suicide.

And an admission of guilt if ever there was one.

He clenched his burning fists and ran further into the woods when suddenly he felt a sharp pain across his right foot and went hurtling through the air.

He landed face flat against the forest floor, which was a whole lot harder and more uncomfortable than he expected. He tasted soggy mud and rusty blood. His bottom lip stung like a bitch. Shit. Landed right on it and bust his lip. Lying in the dirt, in the pouring rain, in the middle of the woods, alone.

So fitting, wasn't it?

He went to stand when he felt a shooting pain up his right ankle.

Fuck. That didn't feel good. Not one bit.

He tried to stand again, but his ankle ached like mad. Just about hobbled to his feet, stood there, tried to walk again, tried to march on through the pain… but damn, it hurt.

He leaned against the damp bark of a tree. Caught his breath. There were no sounds but the hammering rain. No movement approaching.

And yet he felt like he had to keep moving.

He felt like someone was watching.

He went to take a step when suddenly, he spotted something unusual.

A light.

A light. But not behind him. To his left.

Shining directly at him for just a second.

And then, gone.

He stood there. Totally still. And he felt pretty fucking nervous right now. Because seeing a light when you were out in the middle of frigging nowhere was definitely a red flag.

He thought about Eastbrook. Maybe it was someone from home. Maybe they were on his tail.

Or maybe it was someone else.

Stalking him.

Watching him.

He swallowed a lump in his dry throat. Looked around. In the darkness, he saw shapes moving now. Figures. And beyond the pouring rain, he swore he heard whispers.

Whispers getting closer and closer.

He shook his head. Turned around. Kept on walking. His ankle wasn't in a good state at all. But there was no way he was staying put.

He had to keep moving.

He had to get away from whoever the hell was in these woods with him.

Unless...

Suddenly, a weight lifted from his shoulders. Lightning. It must've just been lightning illuminating the woods. Not a torch. Probably just the stress and exhaustion taking it out of him.

Feeling a little more relieved, he hobbled further through the woods. He didn't know where he was heading towards. Didn't have any direction in mind.

But he had to take things one step at a time.

Literally.

He went to lift his dodgy ankle when suddenly he saw something else.

Over to his left.

Something that made the hairs on the back of his neck stand right on end.

That light.

He looked around at it. Saw that beam shining through the woods.

And he knew for certain it wasn't a bolt of lightning anymore.

Somebody was in here with him.

Staring at him.

He looked at that beam.

Looked at the darkness surrounding it.

Stayed really still as the light shone right at him.

He didn't know what to do, whether to say anything, or what to even think.

Just that he was afraid.

Very fucking afraid.

And then, out of nowhere, just like that, the light flickered off again, and darkness surrounded him.

Billy stood there. Totally still. Rain falling heavily. Holding on to the side of a tree.

And as he stood there in the middle of these vast, open woods, a terrifying realisation washed over him.

Someone was following him.

Someone was stalking him.

And it wasn't anyone from Eastbrook.

It was right then that he heard something that filled him with total fear.

From where the light went out, he heard footsteps.

Racing towards him.

CHAPTER NINETEEN

Billy heard the footsteps racing through the darkness towards him, and he didn't have time to think about anything.

He spun around, and he ran.

His ankle ached like mad. Shooting pains shot up his right leg, knocking him sick. He bit his already-bitten lip so hard and ran through the pain, tasting blood. His head was spinning. His heart was racing. His ears were ringing.

He just had to get away.

He ran through the darkness. Ran past the trees. He didn't want to look over his shoulder. Didn't want to see who was pursuing him. He just wanted to get away from them.

And as he ran, his feet squelching through the muddy ground, his breathing heavy, he wasn't even sure if he could hear those approaching footsteps anymore.

But he wasn't stopping.

No frigging way was he stopping.

He wasn't risking it. Wasn't chancing it.

He had to keep going.

Instinctively, without even realising he was doing it, he looked over his shoulder.

Saw nothing but darkness.

Total darkness.

No light.

Nothing.

He turned back around and kept on hobbling as fast as he could through the woods. He might not be able to see anyone, but he knew someone was chasing him. Stalking him. Closing in.

He couldn't stay here.

He had to keep going.

He had no idea how long he'd been running when finally, the pain in his right ankle grew too strong, and he just had to stop.

He leaned against a tree, back right against it. Panting but trying to quieten his breathing. Could he hear footsteps anymore? He wasn't sure. He could only hear his breathing, and the sound of his heart racing, and ringing in his ears, and...

Footsteps.

Right behind him.

Not running anymore.

But walking towards him.

Walking through the woods, right towards him.

He sat still. Totally still. Heart racing faster, which was hard to believe was possible since it already felt like it was about to burst out of his damned chest.

He wanted to get up. Wanted to keep running. Whoever it was, they were chasing him. Fucking with him.

And that wasn't the sort of person he wanted to be dealing with right now.

Not with a knackered ankle.

Not exhausted.

Not with these aching hands of his and the constant agony.

But he did have something.

He reached into his back pocket slowly.

And he pulled out the knife.

The knife that had been used to murder Jorah, presumably. It felt wrong holding it, especially with the intention of using it.

But those footsteps getting closer.

Squelching through the muddy earth.

He calmed his breathing. Sat back against the tree. Knife in hand.

Waited for whoever was pursuing him to appear.

And when they did... he'd defend himself.

He heard the footsteps getting closer.

And as he sat in the darkness, he felt himself return to that garage again.

The darkness of the garage.

The footsteps echoing closer to him.

The laughter.

He gritted his teeth and held onto the knife, and he waited for the footsteps to reach him.

For that light to illuminate him.

But Billy noticed something now.

The footsteps had stopped.

There were no sounds.

Nothing at all.

He waited there. Shaking in the rain. Waited for a sound. Because someone had been following him. They didn't just disappear into thin air like that.

He thought back to the person he'd seen standing in the street back at Eastbrook.

Staring at him.

And he wondered...

Could this person have something to do with whoever that was?

Could it *be* them?

He stayed put for what felt like forever but was probably only minutes, when he realised he had to take this opportunity to get the hell away from here.

To move.

He peeked around the tree.

Saw nothing.

Nothing but darkness.

That was something. That was a start.

Unless they're hiding in the darkness...

He stood up. Got back to his feet. His right ankle was hurting more than ever now. He wasn't gonna be able to run on it. He was going to have to walk. Walk, keep it quiet, and make damned sure he listened out for any signs of life.

He crept across the forest floor, still no direction in sight, just keen to find some sort of shelter, some sort of respite from whoever was pursuing him.

He waded through the mud, keeping it slow, keeping it controlled, keeping it quiet, when suddenly he heard something right behind him.

A branch snapping.

He stopped.

Froze dead in his tracks.

He turned around slowly.

Looked back.

In the darkness, he saw nothing.

Nothing but the alien outlines of the trees.

It's okay. It's in your head. It's in your damned head.

He turned around, and suddenly, out of nowhere, a light illuminated right in front of his eyes, blinding him.

He lifted a hand to cover his face, squinting.

And then he felt a crack across his head, and he fell down to the forest floor.

CHAPTER TWENTY

Darkness.

He was in a garage somewhere. His wrists were tied. Or maybe they were just weak. Maybe he just didn't have any strength in his body. Kind of like when you wake up suddenly in the night and realise you're paralysed. Doesn't matter what you do, and doesn't matter how hard you try, you just can't move. Twitching your little finger is an achievement. Clenching a fist is like climbing Everest.

He didn't know whether he was in this weird stasis right now, where he was, or what was happening.

He just knew he was trapped.

And it felt familiar.

In the darkness, he could see something ahead. A muffled light shining against him, making him squint. He could taste blood on his dry lips. He felt dizzy, and his head felt so heavy. It didn't feel like the nightmares usually felt. The dreams where he realised he was trapped in the garage again. It felt... different, somehow. More muffled. And yet somehow, more *real*.

Like it wasn't a dream.

Wasn't a memory.

Like it *was* real.

He blinked a few times, but his eyes were stinging so bad and so heavy that he decided to keep them closed. If he kept them closed, maybe he'd wake up someplace nice. Maybe he'd wake up in his bed, back at Eastbrook, and Jorah would be alive, and everything would be okay.

Maybe he'd wake up even further back. A child again. A child before the power went out. Making jelly with Grandma. Feeding the ducks with Mum.

And Dad...

Dad...

Stabbing him.

Burying the knife into him.

Seeing that look of betrayal in his eyes as he hobbled over to the church floor.

The memory.

The memory of shame.

The memory of fear.

All rising up and bubbling to the surface and—

Pop.

A pop in his ears.

Like the memories were bubbles, and they were bursting inside his skull.

He was in this dark room. It might be a garage, it might not, but he wasn't sure anymore.

There was a light in front of him, though.

A torch. Shining brightly. Blinding him.

"Where... where am..."

He looked around and realised he was in a rickety wooden chair. His hands *were* tied behind his back. His wrists were bound together. He wasn't in a garage. But it looked like some kind of... some kind of cabin?

He couldn't see anything other than the dusty, dirty wooden floorboards. The mossy walls. The air was so damp it was suffocating.

That light.

That bright light.

He leaned forward to try and free himself from the chair, but his wrists were tied pretty tight. He tried to lift his hands up over his head, dislocating his shoulders in the process if he had to. Whatever it took to get out of this mess.

Someone chasing him through the woods.

Sneaking up on him.

Whacking him over the head and knocking him to the ground.

And then...

Blurry memories.

Blurry memories of someone dragging him.

Carrying him.

The smell of sweat.

And that voice.

A woman's voice.

Muttering things to him.

"...For your own good."

He squinted at that light again when suddenly he realised he wasn't alone.

He couldn't see them properly for the light. But someone was standing behind that torch.

Standing there and staring at him.

Watching him.

He cleared his throat. "What's... what's going..."

"You'd be better off not speaking. Better off not moving at all. Conserve your energy. You're going to need it."

That voice. A woman's voice.

And the more he thought about it, the more he wondered.

Was it a woman's silhouette he saw on the streets in Eastbrook?

It didn't make sense. None of it made sense.

What was happening?

Who was this woman?

"I... My wrists. They're—"

"Tied. Again, for your own good. And for my safety. Although I'm feeling pretty confident seeing the state you're in, I won't lie."

Billy shook his head, spat out a blob of blood on the floor beside him.

"If you'd do your best to avoid spoiling my floor, I'd really appreciate that."

"Yeah, well, if you'd stop shining a light in my face and treating me like a prisoner, I'd appreciate that, too."

The woman didn't say anything to that. Didn't move a muscle.

"What... what do you want with me? Because if you're basically just after torturing me or killing me, I'd really appreciate it if you just got the hell on with it. I've had a pretty shitty few days as it is."

The woman chuckled a little at that. "A man with a sense of humour. Even when he fears for his life. I appreciate that."

"I'm glad I've got something right."

There was more silence. More stillness. Billy had no idea for how long, but it felt like a long time.

But all the time, he tried to free his hands from the ties.

Loosen them.

Break out of them.

But he wasn't finding much luck.

And then the woman walked over to the torch and flicked the light off.

The sudden darkness was almost as disorienting as the intense light.

He saw the woman walking around to face him.

Walking over towards him.

And stopping right before him.

"You ask what I want with you? Why I have you here?"

"It would be pretty helpful, yeah," Billy said. Tugging at those binds around his wrists even more. Feeling them loosen. A chance opening, right before him.

Just had to be careful.

Just had to be patient.

The woman stood there, her dark silhouette staring down at Billy. "You won't believe it. But I've already told you. You're here for your own good. Because it's dangerous out there."

"I think I can handle myself—"

Suddenly, she reached around the back of the chair, grabbed his wrists, and pressed a knife to his throat. "You might think you can handle yourself. But you're complacent. All of you people are complacent."

"You really do have some warm bedside manners, you know?"

The woman tightened her grip on his wrists, just hard enough to make it uncomfortable, and then she let go and stepped back, pulling the knife away from his neck. "You think because you have a cosy little home with nice walls and camaraderie that you're safe. That you're secure. But you've no idea what's on the horizon. Absolutely no idea."

"That sounds to me like a threat."

"Maybe it is," the woman said. "But not from me."

"Really? You're going to pretend you're the good guy here all of a sudden? Knocking me out? Tying me up?"

"I had to be certain."

"Certain of what?"

"That you aren't one of them."

"One of who?"

The woman laughed. Shook her head. "You really do have no idea, do you?"

"If I had an idea, I wouldn't be asking you. One of who?"

She was silent. Just for a moment. But the moment stretched on for what felt an uncomfortably long time.

And then, she broke the silence. "There's a storm coming."

"Sounds ominous."

"You can joke. But you have no idea what's coming for your nice, cosy little community. For your people."

"Wait. Do you know something about Jorah?"

"Jorah? Who's Jorah?"

"He's the leader. Of my community. He was killed... Look, what is all this about?"

The woman shook her head. He still couldn't see her face in the darkness. "Leaders. Followers. All of that will become irrelevant when they arrive on your doorstep."

"When who arrives on our doorstep? What're you talking about?"

She looked at Billy, and lightning flashed outside.

Just long enough for Billy to get a glimpse of her face.

Scarred.

Burned.

"I hope for your sake that you never find out. But you will. You..."

She stopped.

And she turned around.

Because outside, Billy saw something that made the hairs on the back of his neck stand on end.

Lights.

Lights shining in through the dirty windows of whatever this place was.

"They're here," the woman said.

Billy's heartbeat picked up. A sickly taste in his mouth. Fear creeping up, rising again. "Who? Who are here?"

"The storm I told you about," she said. "It's... it's here."

CHAPTER TWENTY-ONE

Billy saw the lights shining through the dirty cabin window, and he felt afraid.

There were three of them. Three that he could see, anyway. Beaming right into the cabin he was inside. The woman who'd captured Billy stood in front of him, totally still, like the proverbial rabbit in the headlights.

He wanted to get out of his chair, but his hands were tied behind his back.

His heart was racing.

And that fear inside him grew more and more intense.

"What—what's happening?" Billy asked. "Who are they?"

The woman didn't respond. She just stood there and stared out at them. For a moment, Billy wondered if she'd frozen completely. If the sight of whoever these people were had paralysed her, like Medusa's victims.

The storm I told you about... it's here.

He remembered those words she'd said to him, and he shuddered.

Who were these people?

What did they want?

And how the hell was he going to get out of this mess?

"I know we haven't exactly got off on the best foot," Billy said, tugging at his wrist ties. "But I'd... I'd really appreciate it if you cut me free right now."

But the woman wasn't budging.

She just stood there. Staring out the window.

Totally still.

The lights flickered through the glass. It felt like they were scanning him and the woman. Like aliens weighing up their prey.

He pulled harder at the ties around his wrists. He needed to get the hell out of here. Whoever these people were and whatever this woman's problem with them was... it wasn't his fight.

All of that will become irrelevant when they arrive on your doorstep...

He thought about what the woman had told him as he tried to pull at the ties, tried to break himself free.

The way she spoke so cryptically about an oncoming threat.

A threat that nobody was safe from.

A storm.

"Hey," Billy said, rocking in his chair now. "Now's really not the time to zone out."

He shook on his chair, realising he had no choice but to take shit into his own hands, when suddenly something happened that filled him with even more fear.

The lights went out.

Darkness filled the cabin.

He sat there. Silent. The only sound was his heart racing, the blood rushing through his head.

"Erm... Hello?" he said. "What's—"

"I need to get out of here," the woman said.

"*You* need to get out of here? I think—I think you're forgetting someone."

"I'm sorry," she said. "But I... I can't do anything more for you. I've got to go."

"No," Billy shouted. "You don't get to just fucking kidnap me then leave me here with... with whoever these people are."

"I'm sorry," the woman said, her dark silhouette right in front of Billy. "But I don't have any choice. There's no time to—"

Right on cue, Billy heard a bang.

Someone bashing right against the door of the cabin.

Hard.

"Fuck!" he said. "Don't just leave me here. You—you can't just leave me here."

The woman rushed across to the side of the cabin and turned back. He couldn't see her face, but he could tell she was looking right at him.

"I'll give you once piece of advice," she said.

"You could give me a fucking *hand*. I'd appreciate that a hell of a lot more."

Another bash on the cabin door. It was going to collapse any moment now. Those people who had this woman so scared, they were going to be in here, and Billy would be alone with them.

"Please," Billy said. "I don't like begging, but I could really do with a hand right now."

"I'm sorry," the woman said. "But... but if I can give you one piece of advice, don't try resisting. Don't try fighting. Don't— don't get your hopes up in any way. I'm sorry. It's over. I... I have to go. I'll do what I can to reach your people and warn them. But... I'm sorry."

"No. Wait. Please!"

And then she was gone.

Just like that, the woman was gone.

And Billy was tied to this chair in the middle of this dark cabin, waiting for whoever the hell this was to bash the door in.

He pulled the ties around his wrists. Tried to stretch them as hard as he could. But it was no use. It was pointless. He was trapped. He was trapped, and he was completely and utterly fucked.

Another bash on the door.

That wood wasn't going to hold much longer.

He closed his eyes, and he thought of Steve.

He thought of Rex.

He thought of Aoife, and he thought of Faye.

You're stronger than you think you are.

You've been through things nobody should ever have to go through, and you've survived...

And then it was Marco he saw in his mind's eye.

Marco, but not Marco as Billy knew him.

Marco as a kid.

Tears rolling down his dirty, bruised face.

Blood trickling from his bust lip.

Looking at Billy in this darkness with fear.

Because they were the same.

They were both the same.

He felt himself back in that garage. Back in the darkness.

He heard the footsteps of the men approaching, getting ready to touch him.

To taunt him.

To beat him.

He heard the footsteps, and he heard the banging, and he felt the fear in the pit of his stomach and his heart racing in his chest and his breathing speeding up, and suddenly, he heard a word as if spoken aloud in his head.

No.

He gritted his teeth.

He pulled his wrists against the ties as hard as he possibly could.

His ankles, too.

He felt the pain.

Sank into the pain.

Sank into it, let it take over him, and let it get stronger and stronger and stronger as the memories filled his head.

Memories of their fingers against his bare flesh.

Of the smell of sour booze on their breaths.

And then the memory of standing over Jorah and burying the knife into him—

No.

No, that wasn't him.

It couldn't be him.

But the memory.

It felt real.

It felt...

Then he felt something.

The ties snapping away from his wrists.

From his ankles.

Agony and freedom.

Freedom *in* agony.

He opened his eyes. Heart pounding. Sitting there in the chair, still in total disbelief.

He heard the door bash again.

Saw the wood crumbling away.

But he was free.

He could get away from this.

Somehow, he was free of the ties, and he had a chance.

He got up from the chair and ran over to the left of the cabin, where the woman disappeared.

Grabbed the door handle with his shaking hand.

A bang.

An almighty crash, right behind him.

He didn't want to look around.

He just wanted to keep on going.

He lowered the handle, swung the door open, and rushed outside.

And as he closed the door, he looked back.

Saw a man standing there.

Grey uniform.

Rifle in hand.

Staring right at Billy.

He saw the man lift the rifle and put his finger on the trigger.

And he turned around and slammed the door shut, and he ran.

Gunshots.

Gunshots cutting through the silent night air.

Footsteps chasing him as he ran into the darkness, shaking, panting, almost laughing with delirium from what just went down.

He ran into the woods.

Ran into the darkness.

Ran towards wherever the fuck he was running towards.

And he didn't stop.

He didn't stop until he was absolutely sure nobody was chasing him anymore.

He didn't stop until he collapsed into a pile of exhaustion and curled up on the forest floor.

He lay there then. Stretched out. Stared up at the treetops and the stars above, and he laughed. He couldn't help himself.

"That was close," he muttered. In shock more than anything. "That was too fucking..."

And then, right on cue, Billy was reminded exactly why he shouldn't get too excited quite so soon.

He heard footsteps.

CHAPTER TWENTY-TWO

Billy heard the footsteps and should've known better than to get too bloody confident about escaping the scary bastards at the cabin.

He lay on the ground in the middle of God knows where in these woods. The stars shone down brightly from above like little spotlights in this endless night. He heard those footsteps getting closer to him, squelching through the mud, and his instinctive reaction?

Keep the hell still.

Keep the hell still and just lie here and hope for the best.

Not exactly his most proactive decision ever, sure. And not exactly his most heroic, either.

But sometimes in life, you just had to know when lying on your arse drenched in mud and waiting for whoever it was to pass by was the right thing to do.

And right now felt like one of those moments.

He closed his eyes. Squeezed them shut. It was stupid, he knew, but it's like when you're a kid and you think that by cutting off your own visual field, you might be more invisible somehow.

And when those footsteps stopped, for a moment, for just a moment, Billy thought maybe it'd worked.

He lay there. Totally still. Other than the fact his body was practically leaping with the way his heart was beating.

He opened his right eye just a little.

Just enough to peek through it.

And when he saw someone standing over him, he regretted it right away.

Fuck.

Someone was here.

They'd caught up with him.

They'd caught up with him and—

"Come on," a voice said. "We can't stay here."

Billy frowned. Wait. That voice. He recognised that voice. And it definitely didn't sound like it belonged to one of those light-waving thugs who'd bashed the cabin door down.

"Hey," the voice said again. A woman's voice. A very familiar woman's voice. "You're lucky to be alive as it is. Don't push your luck. Get the hell up."

And that's when it clicked into place.

The woman who'd kidnapped him.

Who'd tied him up.

And left him behind to die.

It was her.

Before Billy could react in any way whatsoever, she grabbed his arm and yanked him to his feet with surprising strength.

"Ouch," he said. "Don't have to be so rough about it. Jeez."

"Oh, quit whining, you big girl."

"Isn't that sort of comment supposed to be, like, demeaning?"

"It is what it is. Now come on. Let's get the hell away from here."

Billy still couldn't quite believe what was happening. This woman, she'd left him for dead. And now here she was, trying to help him?

It didn't make sense.

She walked through the woods at a surprising speed. And Billy got the sense that if he didn't keep up, it'd just be tough luck.

He ran a little faster, still shaking with the shock of everything and the adrenaline. "Nice of you to leave me behind back there."

"Yeah, I'm sorry for that. It wasn't personal."

"Wasn't personal? Are you actually a full shilling?"

"Look," she said. "Those people are savage, and they kill everything in sight. I really, really didn't fancy dying. You'd have done the same if the roles were reversed. And don't go telling yourself otherwise."

"I..."

But he stopped. Because to be honest? She was probably right.

"I appreciate you coming back for me anyway," Billy said. "I guess."

"Coming back for you? Don't flatter yourself. It's just luck that we ran into each other."

"Charming."

"I'm not known for my bedside manner."

They ran further through the woods. Billy had no idea where they were going, and to be honest, it just felt like they were going nowhere at all.

But whoever this woman was, she clearly had a route in mind.

She clearly knew these woods better than he did.

"I don't even know your name," Billy said.

"What does my name matter?"

"I mean, it'd just be handy to know, that's all. Like, if I'm introducing you to someone, I'd rather not just point at you and go 'that'."

"You won't be introducing me to anyone."

"Do you have to make everything a fucking riddle?"

"I don't make everything a riddle."

"You literally do. 'A storm is coming.' 'The monsters are

approaching your gates.' Come on, Mystic Meg. A name. That's all I want. I'm Billy. And you are?"

A pause. Silence for a few seconds.

And then, "My name is Meg, actually."

Billy laughed. Couldn't help himself. "Of course, it is."

"It's not funny."

"It's kind of funny. I mean, I just called you Mystic Meg, and then you said you're called Meg."

"So hilarious."

Billy shook his head, still smirking. Probably still in shock a bit. This night, it felt like it'd stretched on for bloody forever.

The thought that it was just earlier this night that he'd fled Eastbrook... it just seemed bizarre.

"In here," Meg said.

"In where?"

It took Billy a few seconds to realise where Meg was pointing. But then he saw it. An old motorhome, right in the middle of the woods. Covered in trees and foliage. But a little opening at the front. A door.

"Another hiding place?"

"You need plenty these days."

"There you go with your cryptic shit again."

"You're starting to make me wish I hadn't saved you."

He pushed past the foliage in front of the door of this decrepit old motorhome. Stepped inside. The floor creaked and moved as he walked. It looked like shit in here, from what he could see. Bird shit everywhere. The seats at the table had been torn away. And there was a nasty smell in the air of rotten eggs.

"Nice place," Billy said.

"Nice is just a state of mind."

She looked back at Billy when she said those words.

"Okay," she said. "That was a bit of a cryptic thing to say, I'll admit it."

She sat down at the table, paying no mind to the mould-laden fluff sprouting from the chair. Billy sat opposite her. Didn't want to put his hands on the dirty, muddy table. Didn't want to risk infection one bit.

"So are you going to talk to me straight?" Billy said. "Or are we gonna keep on going down this cryptic route?"

Meg stared at him across the table. He still couldn't see her face properly. Couldn't wait for it to turn light so he could finally put a face to the name. "I figure you've left me with no choice."

"I figure the same. Those people. Who are they? What do they want? And why are you so afraid of them? What do my people need warning about?"

She cleared her throat. Then she leaned across the table. Fidgeted with her hands. "They call themselves the Liberators. And they... they have one goal in mind, and only one goal."

"And what's that?"

"Annihilation," Meg said. "Total annihilation."

CHAPTER TWENTY-THREE

*M*eg held her baby boy in her arms and squeezed her eyes shut. She was in the cupboard under the stairs. Not the safest place in the world, she knew. But right now, it was the safest she could think of. All coats in front of her, shielding her from sight. And coats and throws on top of her and Noah, too, just to protect them even more.

But she didn't feel safe at all.

Not with the sound of gunfire outside.

The sound of crying.

The sound of screaming.

The sound of her community under attack.

She held on to Noah with her shaking hands and rocked him gently from side to side. She was shaking. Frozen. She wanted to reassure Noah. She wanted to tell him everything would be okay.

And she wanted to keep him quiet.

Because if he made a sound, the slightest sound... these people would find her.

They'd find her, and they'd find her boy, and they'd kill them both.

She squeezed her eyes even tighter and rocked Noah from side to side. She tried not to think about the blasts of gunfire. She tried not to think who might be screaming in agony right now. She tried not to think about the footsteps in the house next door, the struggle going down.

She just held on to her baby boy, and she prayed.

It wasn't supposed to be like this. She'd had Noah eight months ago. The dad was a shithead, and he didn't want any responsibility—and you couldn't exactly force him to contribute like you could in the old world.

So, Meg had been forced to raise Noah alone.

But truth be told... she never felt alone. Because her community rallied around her. They helped her. That was the beautiful thing about home. You were never alone here. Everyone worked together. There were no bad eggs, not really. Bar a few twats like George, who should've thought about the fucking consequences of his actions before knocking her up, anyway. Mostly, people here were good. Pure.

And they were all dying.

They were all being slaughtered, one by one.

Her way of repaying them for the help they'd given her?

Hiding in a cupboard under the stairs and praying they didn't find her.

She heard Noah make a little cooing sound, and she covered his lips just a little. "Ssh, baby. Ssh. I've got you. It's okay. It's okay..."

And then she heard something.

Her front door.

Creaking open.

Footsteps.

Someone was inside her house.

She held Noah tight. Kept her hand over his mouth, just a little, as those footsteps got closer.

They were here.

They were here, and they were going to kill her.

They were going to kill her baby.

Noah wriggled around on her shaking knees. He clearly knew something was up. He let out a little cry, which made all the hairs on the back of Meg's neck stand on end.

He couldn't cry.

He couldn't make a sound.

"Ssh," she whispered as the footsteps got nearer.

As they entered the kitchen.

Squeaked across the hard, tiled floor.

She held Noah as tight as she could without hurting him, and she just hoped he'd understand why he had to be quiet. Because if he wasn't quiet, he was dead. They were both most certainly dead.

But Noah was a baby.

He was just a baby, and he didn't understand.

So he kept on wriggling around in her arms.

Trying to break free of her grip.

Trying to cry.

"Please," Meg whispered, tears streaming down her face. "Please, baby. I'm trying to help you. I'm trying to…"

And then she heard something else.

The footsteps.

They were walking around the kitchen.

Walking towards this door.

She held Noah even closer and covered his mouth firmly and hated that she had to do this.

Hated the fear in his little brown eyes.

Hated the sense of betrayal he must feel right now.

She held him close as the footsteps got closer and closer.

And then something happened.

The footsteps.

They started to walk away.

Get further away.

Back towards the hallway.

She felt her shoulders relax, just for a moment.

Felt a wave of relief wash over her.

They weren't out of the woods yet. But she felt like they were going to be okay.

She and her baby were going to be okay.

It was right then that she heard something that made her world fall apart.

Noah let out a high-pitched cry.

She put her hand back over his mouth.

Froze solid.

Held her hand over his lips.

Shit.

Shit, shit, shit.

They must've heard.

They must've heard, and if they'd heard, they'd come back here.

They'd come back, and they'd kill her baby, and they'd kill her.

She sat there. Still. Holding her hand over Noah's mouth and hating every second of it.

Still no footsteps.

Still no sounds.

Just her pulse racing in her skull.

Maybe they were going to be okay.

Maybe the cry wasn't as loud as she thought it was.

Maybe...

Footsteps.

Footsteps marching towards the kitchen.

Marching across the kitchen floor.

Marching over towards the cupboard door under the stairs she was in.

She held Noah even closer.

Felt his warmth against her.

Smelled his soft, sweet skin.

"We'll be okay, baby. We'll be okay. I love you. I love you so much."

And then the door to the cupboard creaked open.

She lay there. Eyes closed.

She didn't want to see.

She didn't want to watch what happened next.

But at the same time, that silence.

That unending silence.

It made her want to look.

It made her want to see.

Like an accident on a motorway. You know you shouldn't look, but you just can't help yourself.

She opened her eyes.

And she saw him standing there.

Rifle in hand.

Staring right down at her.

Right down at her baby.

A man.

A man in grey.

Holding a rifle.

Pointing it at her.

Bright blue eyes and a sweaty bald head.

She looked up at him, and she wanted to fight. She'd been a fighter all her life. Never someone to back down. And never someone to beg.

But right now, holding her boy, a mother's instinct that went beyond everything else kicked in and took over.

"Please," she said. "I'm begging you. Don't do this. Don't do this to my boy. Please."

She looked up into the man's cold eyes.

Listened to the gunshots outside.

To the screams.

Saw that rifle pointed right at her.

"Please," Meg begged. "Please…"

She closed her eyes.

She held her baby close.

She thought about the little laugh he did when she tickled him.

She thought about the nights she'd spent awake, holding him in her arms, rocking him from side to side—and how she wouldn't change a single exhausted minute.

She thought about the dread she'd felt when she discovered she was pregnant.

The time she'd tried sticking a coat hanger up there to deal with the "problem," once and for all.

And how much she regretted even attempting that now.

How much she loved her boy.

Her absolute world.

She held him close to her chest, and she waited for the bullets to hit her when suddenly, she realised she'd been waiting a long time.

Longer than she expected.

She didn't want to open her eyes.

She didn't want to witness the moment she feared so greatly.

But the longer she sat there, eyes closed, holding on to Noah, the more she began to wonder.

She took a deep breath.

Lifted her head just a little.

Opened her eyes, just a peek.

When she opened her eyes, she couldn't believe what she was seeing.

Or rather, what she wasn't seeing.

The man with the gun wasn't standing there anymore.

He was gone.

And for all the chaos surrounding her, she felt one thing in that horrific moment.

Gratitude.

She and her baby were safe.

CHAPTER TWENTY-FOUR

Billy sat in Meg's motorhome and tried to wrap his head around the story she'd just told him.

The sky outside was finally beginning to turn a lighter shade of blue. About time. Billy would be really frigging grateful for the morning. It'd been a hellish night, and he couldn't wait to put it behind him.

But at the same time, the thought of starting a new day in a very new world was terrifying.

There was no going back to Eastbrook. Not now they thought he was Jorah's killer.

And sure, he hadn't exactly helped his case there.

But this right here—stuck in a dingy motorhome with a woman he was ninety-nine per cent sure hated him—was his life now. And he just had to adapt to it.

He could see Meg's face a little better now. She was burned. Her skin was all rough like it was falling to pieces. She kept on picking at loose skin on the backs of her hands. Talking about the past clearly wasn't easy for her. She hadn't made eye contact with him since opening up to him. Not once.

He listened to the birdsong outside. To the silence inside this motorhome. It smelled of mould and damp in here. Made him realise just how much of a luxury life he'd been living back at Eastbrook.

"What happened to your baby?" Billy asked.

Meg looked up at him then. Stared right into his eyes. Her nostrils twitched. And she picked at the skin on the back of her left hand a little harder. "What happened to your *ear*?"

"My ear? Oh." Truth be told, Billy had mostly forgotten about the incident with his ear. Wolf, severing a fair chunk of it from his head. The pain in his hands distracted him from it. And besides, his left ear always used to be a little big, so having a bit shaved off probably wasn't such a tragedy. "Long story. But you're deflecting from your story."

Meg looked away. "I... I walked out of that cupboard under the stairs after... after maybe two days. I didn't want to leave. I could hear screaming all the time. People dying. Begging for their lives. Long after the gunfire stopped. I had to leave eventually because... well. There's no way a woman and a baby can stay somewhere like that forever."

"I'm guessing what you found wasn't pretty."

"Doesn't take a genius to figure that out," she said. "I... I walked out of my house, and I'll never forget how red the sky was. And how... how much worse it made everything feel. My people. People in the streets. Kids. Kids as—as young as three. It didn't matter. They just walked through, and they slaughtered them."

"Shit," Billy said.

"I survived because I was lucky. Because—because one of them had a crisis of faith, or whatever. But Noah and I... we weren't supposed to make it out. We were already blessed by the fact we were living."

"Where did you go from there?"

"I did what any single mother would do. I tried to find my baby a new home. And I found somewhere. Somewhere nice. Only... Well. You can guess what happened."

"Liberators," Billy said.

Meg nodded. "Came in. Swept through the place, just like they did the last place. Only... only I wasn't as lucky this time."

She looked away. He saw her burned face in the moonlight now. He didn't want to ask any more questions. He didn't need to know.

But she carried on anyway.

"They killed Noah right in front of me," she said, her voice cracking. "Took him from my arms and shot him like—like he was nothing."

"I'm sorry."

"And then—and then they raped me. They raped me, eight of them, and then they beat me. And they cut me. Me and—and so many others. I thought I was going to die. I *wanted* to die. And then... and then by chance, by some drop of the ball or whatever, I got away. Another chance."

"And I'm guessing you've been out here ever since?"

"I've been watching them ever since," Meg said. "I... I don't know what I hoped to gain. Maybe by watching them, I could plan revenge. Or—or I could at least warn another group. Another community. To stop the same thing happening to them."

"I'm guessing that's why you're here. Telling me."

"The place you call Eastbrook is in their sights. It's next in their path. And based on everything I've seen... they are planning to attack soon. Very soon."

"Fuck."

"They follow a pattern. Destabilising existing order through interception. They love to get people afraid. To get people weak. And then when morale is low, they love to sweep right in and destroy a community while it's down."

"Interception..." Billy said. "The—the leader. Jorah. He was murdered."

"That sounds like something the Liberators would do. Via someone on the inside."

"They—they're trying to pin it on me, somehow. Why me?"

"I don't know that. But it's like I say. There will be people on the inside who you think you know well. You might even think you love them. But they don't have your best interests at heart."

"Why would anyone betray us like that?"

"Because they've been promised something far greater."

"What could be greater than what we've got?"

Meg shook her head. "Power. A better future. Who knows? Promises can be strong. And just because you're content doesn't mean everybody is."

"But this is... this is genocide. I can't think of anyone who'd stand by something like that. Like, I have people I don't get on with. But this..."

Meg sighed. "I'm sorry to say, but someone isn't who you think they are. And besides. You need to get past that now. Because it really doesn't matter. What matters is far more urgent."

"Far more urgent?"

"Warning your community. Warning your community to brace themselves. Because the Liberators are on the horizon. And their attack is imminent. Or your entire community and everyone you care about will be destroyed."

CHAPTER TWENTY-FIVE

By the time the sun rose, Billy hadn't had a wink of sleep.

How in hell's name was he supposed to sleep when he knew what was on the horizon?

It was bloody boiling inside this motorhome. So damned stuffy. He'd sat on the chair by the window all night, which was far from comfortable. The material was all torn, and the innards were spilling out of it like a cushiony disembowelling had gone down.

Meg sat opposite him. Her eyes were closed. She wasn't awake yet. He'd spent the morning just watching her. Watching the rising sun illuminate her burned face.

He thought about the pain she'd been through. The pain of losing her community. The pain of losing her son.

And as much as Billy felt a bit pissy with her for dragging him into a shitty situation and almost leaving him for dead, he couldn't blame her.

And besides. He knew the truth now.

The truth about the people she called the Liberators.

What their goal was.

Annihilation.

He looked out of the window towards the woods. The green

trees. Rabbits running around, blissfully unaware that they might well be breakfast. The motorhome smelled of sweat and damp. His mouth was dry. He felt groggy, and his eyes were burning. He couldn't remember the last time he'd slept. Felt like a dark cloud was hanging over him, constantly.

Especially now he knew what he had to do.

Eastbrook. It was in imminent danger. Someone had taken Jorah out to destabilise the place, and now it was next in line to be crushed by the Liberators.

And here Billy was. On the run. Out here in the woods in the wake of a murder. Prime suspect.

And Eastbrook had no idea what was coming.

He thought about what he'd have to do. He'd have to go back there and warn them. He had no other choice.

But he was wanted for a death. What did he expect to do? Just wander in and for the people to welcome him with open arms?

No. They'd think he was full of shit. Marco already suggested he was losing his mind...

Marco.

Could it be him?

Could he be the traitor?

He remembered seeing him right after he'd seen the figure in the street last night, and he wondered.

He looked back around and saw Meg staring at him.

"Oh," Billy said. "You're awake."

"I've been awake for hours."

"Didn't look that way."

"I like to meditate a little in the morning. Clear my head. Want breakfast?"

"I... I'm not sure time's really gonna allow for breakfast, is it?"

"Nonsense," Meg said. She got up, walked over to a rather sticky-looking fridge peppered with dirt and mould. She opened it, and immediately, a horrid rotting smell filled the motorhome.

Flies buzzed everywhere. It was so grim in there that Billy couldn't even figure out what was what.

But Meg grabbed some container in a plastic bag—seeming rather unfazed by the godawful smell—closed the fridge door, and planted the bag on the table.

She pulled a container out of it, then cracked open a lid, and suddenly the smell of rot was replaced by a much nicer smell.

"Chicken?" Meg asked.

Billy looked down at the container of rather lush, lean looking chicken. And amazingly, as much as he was pretty curious about the food hygiene practices in this place, he reached and grabbed a piece. Chewed it. Wow. It was juicy and damned delicious. Melted in his mouth. He didn't realise just how hungry he was. "You're a good cook."

"Thanks. I've had to learn a thing or two about cooking. I guess we all have, right?"

Billy chewed another piece of that succulent chicken. Nodded. "I guess so."

But the second he swallowed that piece of chicken, a sense of dread picked up inside him.

Of inevitability.

"I... I need to warn my people," Billy said.

He stood up. Walked over the creaky motorhome floor, across to the door.

"You're in the middle of nowhere, respectfully," Meg said. "You're probably going to need my help."

"You said time was of the essence. Shouldn't we be moving?"

Meg nodded. "We should. But it's important to eat, also. To be hydrated. We make a lot of silly, careless errors when we're not—"

"Are you for real?" Billy asked.

"What?"

"You told me my community is in danger of being wiped out. You told me you'd watched two communities fall. Your own..." He stopped himself short of saying "son", just in time. "You've lost. Big time. And now you're saying we should take our time?"

"It's early," Meg said. "And there's a long day ahead of us. A long journey, first. And then... well. It isn't going to be straightforward for your people. Leaving their home. They probably aren't going to be keen on the idea. Probably overestimate their defensive capabilities. Even if you're a respected member of that community, convincing them to walk away from everything they hold so dear isn't going to go down a treat."

"What if I'm not a respected member of the community?"

"Well. I guess we can only work with the hand we're dealt, right?"

Billy shook his head. Turned away. "They're not going to believe a word I say."

"And that's a problem."

He stood at the door. He didn't know what the fuck he was going to do. He had no fucking clue how any of this was going to go. But he knew one thing for sure.

He was going to go back to Eastbrook.

He *had* to warn them about what was coming.

He *had* to make them believe.

Because there were people he loved there.

People he cared about more than anything on the planet.

He looked back at Meg. "I'll figure it out."

She nodded at him. Chewed another piece of that chicken. "I should hope you do," she said. "Because if you don't... you can say goodbye to everything you've ever cared about. Because it's over."

CHAPTER TWENTY-SIX

Marco followed the footprints through the woods, and he knew he was close.

It was a stuffy morning. Really muggy, really humid. Last place he wanted to be right now was out here in the woods. You'd think it'd be cooler, somehow. The leaves dampening the sun somewhat.

But it wasn't. In the height of summer, the leaves kept the heat *in*.

But it didn't matter. None of it mattered.

Because he felt like he was getting close.

He looked at the pair of footprints on the muddy ground. He'd been following them for a while now. He'd lost sense of how long he'd been walking, but definitely since just before sunrise—which made it early at this time of year.

He listened to the birds singing above, and it reminded him of those darker times.

The times he'd been locked away.

The times he'd been trapped in that dark garage.

His only escape was the sounds of the birds singing above him.

He used to dream he was out there. Floating in the sky amongst them. Flapping his wings. And those dreams would feel so real. They'd feel so perfect. And he'd feel so happy as he waded through the sky, away from the hell below.

But then he'd wake up.

Wake up to the sound of a metal door rattling against the brick wall of the place he was in.

Or to the smell of cigarette smoke and alcohol.

The fear that came with it.

The fear that *always* came with it.

He remembered those things, and he thought of Billy.

There was a twinge of sadness in the centre of his chest when he thought of Billy. Because he'd been hiding the truth for years.

The truth that he knew what Billy had gone through.

That he knew Billy had gone through the same hell as him.

And he knew what that sort of hell could do to a person. He knew how much it could take out of you. How much it could *break* you.

But then he remembered what Billy had done.

How he'd murdered Jorah.

And as much as he sympathised with the horrors he'd been through—as much as he was finally beginning to see why he'd been so resistant about Billy for so many years because he reminded him of his own horrifying past—there was no getting away from the brutal nature of Billy's actions, and how dangerous it made him.

He'd murdered Jorah.

He'd absolutely destroyed him.

And yet...

He remembered finding Billy in the street. Remembered finding him with that knife in his hand.

And as much as everything looked like it just... well, added up, there was still a sense deep inside Marco that everything wasn't quite as it seemed.

That there was more to this than appeared on the surface.

Or maybe that was just him.

Maybe that was just his usual overthinking ways going into overdrive once again.

Maybe he needed to stop overthinking and just recognise the facts right before him, as clear as day.

Billy had murdered Jorah.

He'd caught him wandering the streets with the murder weapon.

And then he'd watched him flee.

What clearer signal of guilt did he need?

He shook his head. Walked further through the woods, following these prints—prints he knew might well lead to nowhere.

And then he stopped.

Because he saw something.

Something right in front of him.

An old motorhome.

It wasn't in good condition. It was covered with leaves and vines. The white paint was cracking away, and it was mostly all rust at this point.

But what was inside the motorhome froze Marco in his tracks.

Because standing at the door of the motorhome, Marco saw something.

Someone.

Someone he recognised very well.

Standing at the door to the motorhome, Marco saw Billy.

He crouched.

Hid in the bushes.

He had him right where he wanted him.

CHAPTER TWENTY-SEVEN

Billy walked through the woods after Meg, and he couldn't shake the feeling he was being watched.

It was pretty typical. I mean, he knew it was pretty fucking normal to feel this way, right? The trees were thick as hell all around him. And other than the singing of the birds and his footsteps squelching through the mud, everything was so silent.

He watched Meg walk through the woods far quicker than he was comfortable with. Not that he could have a go at her for that. Time was of the essence, after all. His community was in danger. Under great threat. If anyone should be rushing, it should be him.

But there was just that niggling feeling someone was following.

And also the fear of what he was going to be greeted with when he got home.

Nothing good, that was for sure.

"Do you even want to save your people?" Meg asked, turning around and sighing.

"What?"

"You're hardly striking me as particularly urgent right now. Some would say you're stalling."

"I'm just... I'm doing my best, okay? Clearly not as swift a mover as you."

"Yeah, well, maybe you should try speeding up a little."

"Do you *think* I'm meaning to walk slowly?"

"It wouldn't stun me."

Billy looked back over his shoulder. He looked through the trees. He could smell sweat, presumably from himself—a smell he'd grown pretty accustomed to over the years. But it seemed particularly strong today.

Was he crazy, or did he smell someone else's sweat, too?

"Weird question," Billy said. "But would you mind if I sniffed your armpit?"

Meg stopped. Looked around. Frowned. "You know, if anything, I thought you might be a bit vanilla when I first met you. Armpit fetish is definitely not what I had in mind."

"I know it sounds weird."

"Yeah. It does sound weird. And it's a no, by the way."

"I just... I can smell someone. Someone who isn't me. I guess I just wanted to rule out..."

He saw the way she was looking at him, and he knew it was probably a good idea to back the hell off right now.

"No. You're right. Course it's a no. Sorry."

She raised an eyebrow and turned around. "Don't worry. I'd know if someone was close."

"You got Spidey-Senses too?"

"I just... Spend long enough time out here in the woods on your own, and you grow pretty accustomed to when someone's lurking. Come on. We need to get a move on. Unless, like I said, you don't *want* to save your people."

Billy nodded. He caught up with Meg a little. Walked alongside her. He didn't know what to say to her. He felt like he knew surprisingly little about her, but at the same time, things he wasn't supposed to know.

The truth about her past.

About her son.

About the horrors she'd suffered at the hands of the Liberators.

"These people," Billy said. "The Liberators. There's something I can't wrap my head around about them."

"Oh yeah?"

"It's just... hear me out. But I don't understand why they'd do what they do. What their aims are."

"Destruction. Like I told you."

"But that's not a *reason*. That's not an *aim*. What do they want? Really?"

Meg shrugged. "I don't see why it matters, really."

"Of course, it matters."

"You think?"

"If you can figure out *why* someone's doing something, if you can understand the motive, then you can maybe understand... I dunno. What it takes to stop them."

Meg tilted her head. "That's nice. Really. I mean, that's real good pop psychology right there. But truth is, sometimes the world doesn't work that way, pet. Sometimes, people just want to bring the whole thing down. If you spend too much time pulling your hair out trying to figure out why, you're wasting time."

Billy nodded. He didn't agree. But in a way, Meg was right. What did it matter right now? The Liberators were on the horizon. They were closing in. And Eastbrook was in danger. Big danger.

Stopping that immediate threat was his primary goal.

It had to be his primary goal.

Everything else came second to that.

"We get to your place. You tell them what's coming. Hopefully, they listen. After that... well. That's up to them."

"And what about you?" Billy asked.

"What about me?"

"Are you going to help me?"

"My help is delivering the message. But I have to survive. Because I have to warn other people. Other groups. And if I can warn enough, before it's too late... maybe we can work towards forming a group big enough to take them on."

"How's that recruitment drive going so far?"

"Honestly? You're the first."

"Excellent."

"We'll get there," Meg said. "I... I refuse to lose hope. The second I lose hope, it's over. I might as well kill myself. All of us might. But... but if there's hope, there's a chance."

"Who's the pop psychologist now?" Billy said.

"Shut up."

She smiled. And when she smiled, Billy smiled back at her. Must be the first time the pair of them exchanged a smile.

And it felt nice, in a way.

It felt... hopeful.

"Thank you for not judging me for leaving you behind," Meg said. "Not a lot of people would look past that."

"Who says I haven't judged you?"

She looked back at him.

Right into his eyes.

Smiled again.

And he smiled back at her.

They stood there in the silence of the woods together.

United in grief.

"Come on," Meg said. "Let's..."

She stopped.

Her face dropped.

Billy didn't realise why.

Not until he heard the footsteps on either side of him.

Not until he heard movement closing in.

He looked around, and he saw a man standing there.

Pistol in hand.

A man he recognised.

"Marco," he said.

"On the ground, Billy," he said. "Don't make this difficult. It's over."

CHAPTER TWENTY-EIGHT

"No fucking around, Billy. On the ground, right this second. Your friend here, too. Don't make this any harder than it already is."

Billy saw Marco standing there with the pistol in his hand, and he should've known to trust his frigging gut.

He knew someone was watching him. Following him. If he hadn't listened to Meg, who *insisted* her Spidey-Senses alerted her to the presence of any fucker, he might've kept a lower profile.

Instead, he was staring down the gun barrel of probably his least favourite Eastbrook resident—and the Eastbrook resident who liked him least.

Just typical really, wasn't it?

He looked around at Meg. Saw Harvey, one of Marco's mates, pointing a pistol at her, too. She looked back at Billy with anger in her eyes. Which was rich, really, considering *she* was the one who claimed she'd know when someone was snooping about.

"I really didn't want to have to do this," Marco said. "But you've left me with no choice."

"Oh, don't give me that crap," Billy said. "You've wanted to nail me for years."

"That's not true, Billy."

"Wouldn't even surprise me if you're the one who framed me. Who killed Jorah."

"Billy," Marco said. "You're losing your grip. This is for your own good. And for the good of everyone at Eastbrook."

"I'm sure it is."

"The council has voted unanimously in favour of your capture and imprisonment. Even Steve. What does that tell you?"

It stung, he had to admit. But at the same time, it was hardly surprising, was it? He knew how it looked. And it was very rare for the council *not* to vote unanimously on matters.

It was just a bump in the road as far as Billy was concerned.

But a non-negotiable one that hurt like hell.

"Look," Billy said. "I won't lie to you. I know exactly what it looks like. But—"

"Get on your knees, Billy. Right this second."

He looked at Marco, and he wanted to punch his lights out for stalling him like this.

But instead, he knew that if he wanted Marco on side—if he wanted to stand any chance of preventing the attack on East-brook—he would have to play by Marco's rules a little.

So he did what he hoped he'd never have to do for Marco.

He got down onto his knees.

"That's it," Marco said, walking over to him. "That's more like it."

"Marco," Billy said. "There's—there's someone out there trying to destroy our community."

"Heard it all, Billy. Heard it all."

"It's true," Meg said.

Marco looked around at Meg. Frowned. "Who is this?"

"Her community was destroyed by the people who want to destroy our home. They—they call themselves the Liberators. They want nothing more than to see us all fall. To see *all* our communities fall. And they're coming for us next. Stoking division. Fear. And then... and then they're going to attack, and it's going to be brutal. Unless we get people away. Unless we buy ourselves some more time."

Marco stared at Billy. Then looked over at Meg again. His cheeks looked flushed. It was hard to tell what he was thinking right now. Which Billy found worrying. Because he had no idea where he stood.

"I know it sounds far-fetched," Billy said. "I know—I know it sounds bordering on the ridiculous. But... but Meg's been there. She's been there, and she is trying to warn us. She is trying to help us. We have to listen to her. We have to hear her out. Or... or it might be too late already."

Marco looked down at Billy, and Billy could see how torn he was now. How conflicted he was.

He hoped he'd spoken to him.

He hoped he'd struck a chord.

But then Marco took a deep breath, and he sighed. "We're going to take you back to Eastbrook. Both of you. And then we can hear what you've got to say and decide what we're going to do with you."

He walked over to Billy and went to whack a pair of cuffs around his wrists.

"Wait!" Billy said, shooting to his feet.

Marco held his ground, pointed the pistol at Billy. "Get back down."

"We don't have time to talk about it," Billy said. "We—we don't have time to mull over what to do. That's what—that's what they want. They want to catch us off guard. They want to catch us in a moment where we don't know what the hell is going on. A moment of grief. We need to act. We need to act as soon as possible. Or... or before we know it, it'll already be too late."

Marco shook his head. "I say this with the greatest respect because I've been there. But... but you murdered Jorah. You murdered him, and you did a runner."

"Because I knew what would happen to me if I stayed. And it's a good job I did, now I know the truth—"

"You're deluded," Marco said. "You're... you're deluded because you're broken. By the things that have happened. By the things you've been through. And I'm sorry you've been through those things. I'm sorry you've suffered. But... but the things you've done can't go unnoticed. The pain you've caused cannot go unpunished. And you aren't going to be the one calling the shots. You just aren't. So get back on your knees. Now."

Billy stared into Marco's eyes.

He wanted to plead to his better nature.

He wanted to win him over. To make him see the truth.

But in the end, there was nothing he could say to Marco.

He knew he was already too far gone on that front.

There was no convincing Marco of his side of the story.

And that had dangerous ramifications for Eastbrook.

"Get down on your knees, and this ends," he said. "We go home. We figure out an appropriate punishment for you. And we get you the help you need."

Billy stood there, and he shook his head. It couldn't end like this. Everything hadn't built to this moment to end so drastically like this.

"I can't," Billy said.

Marco sighed. "Then you leave me with no choice."

A bang.

The sound of a gunshot.

Billy closed his eyes.

CHAPTER TWENTY-NINE

Billy heard the gunshot rattle through the woods, and he expected to feel pain in the middle of his chest.

He expected agony. He expected non-existence. He expected darkness.

But, strangely, that didn't happen.

Instead of non-existence, Billy could still perceive what was going on.

He could still see the darkness behind his closed eyes.

He could still hear that gunshot ringing in his skull.

He could still taste the sweat on his lips and feel his heart thumping at dangerous speeds.

Which could only mean one thing.

The bullet hadn't hit him.

Marco hadn't pulled the trigger.

So who had?

He opened his eyes.

Marco stood opposite him.

But his pistol wasn't pointed at Billy anymore.

It was pointed past him.

Behind him.

He looked around.

Saw Meg staring into the woods.

Fear in her eyes.

And then he saw something else.

Something that filled him with fear.

Harvey was clutching his neck. It was bleeding—badly. Spurting blood right through his shaking fingers.

And upon seeing him like that, Billy felt cold.

Very, very cold.

Because if it wasn't Marco or Harvey who'd pulled the trigger, and if it wasn't Meg who'd pulled the trigger, and it wasn't *him* who'd pulled the trigger...

Who was it?

It was someone else.

Meg looked around at him, and she shook her head.

"I'm sorry," she said.

And then she ran off into the woods.

Billy stood there. Stood with Marco opposite him. Silent.

Total silence, but for Harvey's gargling, gasping, struggling.

He looked around at Marco, and Marco looked back at him.

"What..." Marco started.

And then he heard another bang.

More bangs.

From the right.

And before he had time to think, before he could stop to consider what he was doing, he ran.

He ran, and Marco ran with him.

Bullets peppered past him, slamming into the bark of the trees.

He felt them whooshing past him.

Narrowly missing him.

Kept on running.

Kept on going.

They were here.

The Liberators were here, and they were going to kill him before he had a chance to warn Eastbrook about them.

Meg had done a runner—again. And he couldn't blame her.

But at the same time, he didn't trust that she would get to Eastbrook in time to warn them—or if she'd be able to convince them of the truth.

He could only run right now.

Run through the woods.

Run through the trees.

Run as those bullets kept on whizzing past.

Closer and closer to connecting with him.

He looked around at Marco, who ran alongside him.

"Believe me now?" Billy said.

Marco didn't say anything back.

He just kept on running.

Billy ran alongside him as those bullets kept on flying past. He didn't know where he was going. Only that it didn't feel like he was getting any further away from the attackers. He didn't know which way Eastbrook was. He was lost. Very fucking lost.

And being lost was not a good place to be when you were being hunted down by a frigging death cult.

He looked over his shoulder. Couldn't see them.

Just the trees.

The leaves.

The branches.

And then bullets.

Bullets whizzing past.

Banging.

He turned ahead, and he saw an opening.

A clearing up ahead.

Sun shining down.

And...

A deer?

Was that a deer standing there?

Watching?

It seemed too still.

It seemed too fucking bizarre.

It seemed...

He felt something, then.

Right beneath his feet, he felt the ground give way.

Felt himself tumble down.

Crack his face against the earth.

Slam against the ground.

Marco landing right beside him.

"Fuck," Billy said, spitting dirt. "What the..."

He looked up.

Saw an opening above.

Heard the footsteps above.

The Liberators were going to find them down here.

They were going to find them in this hole in the ground, and they were...

And then something struck Billy.

This hole.

It wasn't natural.

The walls were made from wood.

And that hole above...

It was like a trapdoor.

Like someone was *supposed* to fall down here.

Suddenly, out of nowhere, the opening slammed shut.

Darkness filled the room they were in—wherever it was.

Billy sat there. Aching like mad, especially his shoulder. He sat alongside Marco, and he stayed still. They both stayed still. Very still.

They listened to the footsteps creaking across the roof.

Listened to them all running by.

And as he sat there, as much as he knew falling through a bloody trap door wasn't exactly ideal, he felt a sense of relief.

Whoever had opened that door, they'd done him a favour.

A big favour.

"What... what is this place?" Marco asked.

Billy looked around.

Looked at the wooden walls, barely visible in the darkness.

Looked at that opening above.

And then he heard footsteps across from him.

Heading his way.

He turned around.

Looked into the darkness.

Saw someone approaching him.

Someone holding a match.

He stood there. Still. Very still.

Heart racing.

Shaking.

Waiting for them—whoever they were—to reach him.

They stopped.

Stopped right in front of him.

Stood there, holding that match.

"Well?" Billy said. "Are you just gonna stand there, or are you gonna tell us how fucked we are?"

The man laughed.

"Oh, I am," he said.

He stepped closer to Billy.

Lifted the match to his face.

And when Billy saw who it was... his stomach sank.

"Oh," Billy said.

"Oh, indeed."

Because he knew the man standing before him.

He knew exactly who he was.

"Jarrod," Billy said.

CHAPTER THIRTY

If there's one person Billy really didn't want to run into when he was fleeing from a death cult, it was probably the man standing opposite him.

"Jarrod," Billy said.

Jarrod stood there holding a match to his face. His beard was long and scruffy, peppered with greys. The makeshift walls of this weird underground layer flickered in that dim light. Above, Billy didn't hear any footsteps or gunshots anymore.

Just his heavy breathing.

Marco's heavy breathing.

And Jarrod's heavy breathing.

It smelled down here. Bad. Sweat. Shit. Piss. The entire happy array of delightful scents. The stench was so bad he could practically taste it.

And as he looked into Jarrod's bloodshot eyes, he felt the darkness of this little den closing in.

The last time he'd seen Jarrod, he'd watched his daughter, Jade, die at the hands of Wolf.

Jarrod fell to the ground. Let out a haunting cry.

And as much as Billy detested everything he'd heard about the man—Ramiro's great rival, his conqueror and the man who'd been responsible for horrors involving Marco, too—he couldn't help feeling sympathy for anyone who'd lost a daughter like he had.

"I knew you'd come," Jarrod said. "I—I knew you'd come back to me."

Billy glanced around at Marco, who stood beside him, eyes reflecting in that flickering light. Saw him staring at Jarrod. He looked frozen.

Frozen with fear.

Billy looked back at Jarrod. At the sores on his face. At how much more emaciated he looked than when he'd last seen him, even though not much time had passed at all, in the grand scheme of things.

He looked haunted. Cut a ghostly figure.

And again, as much as this man was responsible for all kinds of horrors, Billy couldn't help feeling a hint of sympathy for him.

"I—I waited. Waited for you. To drop down from above. I knew you would. We—we both knew you would. Didn't we, Jade? Didn't we?"

He turned around to the darkness, and Billy caught a whiff of a new smell. Something awful. Something even worse than the piss, and the shit, and the sweat.

Something... rotten.

"We... we really need to go," Billy said.

"Go?" Jarrod said. Match shaking between his fingers. "Why would you go? After everything, after all our waiting, why would— why would you go?"

The sadness in his eyes.

The shaking of his lips.

One thing was for sure.

Jarrod wasn't completely here. Not anymore.

He'd lost his mind.

And that made for an even more sensitive situation than Billy expected.

"Look," Billy said, backing up just a little. He didn't know how they were going to get out of here. That trap door, seemed too high to climb up out of. There had to be another way out. Another escape route. "We... we appreciate a reunion as much as the next person. But—"

"You—you aren't even going to say hello to Jade?"

A bitter taste filled Billy's mouth. "Jade's... Jade's gone, Jarrod."

Jarrod glared at him. His eyes narrowed even more. Billy swore he saw a tear trickle down his cheek. "Gone?"

"She's... I'm sorry. But she's gone. The Animals. The people in the wolf masks. They... I'm sorry."

Jarrod shook his head. Started staggering around the confines of this hole. "Gone. Gone. Gone. No. Can't be gone. Can't be gone."

And seeing him distracted, Billy nudged Marco. "We need to get out of here."

But Marco was still.

Marco was unmoving.

"Marco," Billy said. "We need to—"

"He raped me," Marco said.

Billy heard the words and felt a heavy weight crash down on his shoulders. "What?"

"When I was a child, he raped me. And he... he made me think it was going to stop. He kept telling me he was going to stop. Making me think it was over. Making me think I was safe. And then he'd do it again. Just when I thought I was safe. He—he raped me."

Hearing these words made Billy's skin turn cold.

The darkness of the garage.

The touch against his skin.

And the memory of those men, and what they did to him too...

"I'm... I'm sorry," Billy said.

"He has to suffer."

"We have to go."

But Marco wasn't listening.

Marco was possessed by something else entirely.

"He has to suffer," he said.

He walked over towards Jarrod, who paced around from side to side, when suddenly he heard something above.

Footsteps.

Footsteps and voices.

They were coming back.

The Liberators were out there, and they were searching the area.

They needed to be quiet down here.

So quiet.

Fuck.

He looked up.

He had no idea where they were walking.

But he knew they were close.

"Marco," Billy whispered. "They're—they're back. We need to..."

But Marco stood opposite Jarrod.

He stood opposite him, fists clenched, pistol in hand. Tears rolling down his face.

"This is for my childhood," Marco said.

"Marco, no!"

"This is for all of us."

It all happened so fast.

Marco went to pull the trigger.

Jarrod spun round.

His eyes widened.

And just before Marco could pull the trigger, Jarrod punched his hand and threw Marco down to the ground.

Only Marco *wasn't* too late pulling the trigger.

A deafening gunshot rattled out of his pistol like an explosion in Billy's ears.

He stood there. Stood there as Jarrod stood over Marco, who lay on the ground, trying to get back to his feet.

He stood there as his ears rang, unable to hear a thing.

He stood there, and then as his hearing began to return, he heard something that filled him with total dread.

Footsteps.

Running this way.

The Liberators were coming.

CHAPTER THIRTY-ONE

Billy heard the Liberators closing in on him again, and he knew this wouldn't be an easy situation to get himself out of.

His ears were ringing like mad after the gunshot. In the darkness, he saw Jarrod and Marco wrestling with one another. Jarrod had Marco pinned to the ground. He was shouting inaudible things at him. Punching him. Kicking him.

And Billy knew he had to get out of here.

He couldn't get caught up in whatever scrap they had going on.

Especially not with the noise they were making and the attention they were drawing to themselves.

He looked around in the darkness. Up towards the trap door, which a little light shone through. And then across, over towards where Jarrod appeared from.

He had no idea what this place was, how big it was, or how far it went.

But he knew he needed to get away.

He knew he needed to get out of here.

The future of Eastbrook depended on it.

He went to run down the darkened corridor of dirt when he saw Jarrod pinning Marco down, strangling him, crying.

"You can't go," he said. "You can't—you can't just go."

But it wasn't Jarrod he felt pity for anymore. He might well be too far gone. He might've lost in a serious way.

But hearing what Marco told him just before.

About Jarrod abusing him.

He didn't feel hatred towards Marco anymore.

He felt pity towards him.

He understood what he'd been through. And why he was so reluctant for any kind of closeness with Billy.

He understood.

He walked over to them when he heard something above.

Banging.

Footsteps.

So close now.

He looked down.

Looked down and saw Marco on his back.

Saw Jarrod tightening his palms around his throat, squeezing his windpipe.

He saw Marco's bloodshot eyes.

The drool trickling from his lips.

And then he saw the pistol lying by his side.

He knew he had to get away.

He knew that by leaving Marco and Jarrod here, he could buy himself some time—and kill two birds with one stone, so to speak.

But... no.

He reached down, grabbed the pistol, and pointed it at the side of Jarrod's head.

"This is for all of us," Billy said.

He pulled the trigger.

A click.

But no bang.

Jarrod swung around.

Glared at him.

"Oh," Billy said. "Of course. Of fucking course."

And before he had time to react, Jarrod was on his feet, punching him in the gut, knocking him to the muddy ground.

The full force of his body pressing down against him.

"You killed my daughter," he shouted. "You—you killed my Jade."

And hearing those words, interspersed with the punches to his face, Billy remembered exactly how it went down.

Refusing to kneel.

Wolf killing Jade.

Stabbing her in front of him and telling Billy it was on him.

"You killed her," Jarrod shouted.

Punching.

Punching.

Punching.

"You killed her!"

Billy looked up at Jarrod as he lay on his aching back, and he saw his fist raised in the air.

Ready to deliver a blow to his face.

A blow that he knew damn well might be the last he ever felt.

"No," Billy said, spitting out blood. "I didn't... I didn't kill her. Life... life just caught up with you."

He saw Jarrod's face turn.

Saw the anger turn to horror.

Like he was realising exactly what Billy was suggesting—and realising it was the truth.

He went to swing his fist when suddenly, Billy heard another bang.

Felt blood splatter all over his face.

Blood and fragments of skull.

The taste of metal.

He lay there as Jarrod fell on top of him.

As his weight squeezed the air from his lungs.

He tried to move him.

Tried to wriggle free of him.

Wondered where the hell Marco had gone.

He went to push Jarrod's body away when suddenly he noticed something.

Right in front of him.

Someone walking over to him.

He lay there on his back, heart racing, and he went completely still.

There was someone in the den with him.

Holding a rifle.

Walking his way.

A Liberator.

illy lay on the ground, completely still, as the Liberator approached.

He watched his silhouette approach in the darkness, rifle in hand. Walking towards him slowly. He lay there, heart racing, the weight of Jarrod's dead body pushing down on his chest, suffocating him. He could feel his warm blood trickling onto his face; taste its rustiness on his lips.

His ears rang.

His head spun.

He needed to get out of this mess.

But what the hell was he supposed to do?

Pinned down.

Cornered.

And that Liberator was getting closer, closer.

He lay there, shaking. The Liberator was just inches away now. Looking down at him. Or at Jarrod. He couldn't tell. Probably a combination of both.

And as he lay here, he wondered where Marco was. Didn't blame him for running, even if it was fucking typical. The reason

Billy was lying here in the first place was 'cause he tried to save Marco.

How had Marco repaid him?

By running the fuck away.

But again, he couldn't exactly hold it against him. He would've done the same.

He almost did the same.

He *should've* done the same.

And now he was lying here facing up to the consequences of his actions.

The Liberator stopped, right over him. Billy just kept still. Those were his instincts. Stay still and hope to God the Liberator didn't see him lying here in the darkness.

But he'd seen the torches they had last night.

He'd seen them shining through the windows of Meg's cabin.

He thought about Meg. Wondered where the hell she was at right now.

Fuck, this was a shitshow. The whole damned thing was a shitshow.

He lay there, and he stayed still, and he waited for the Liberator to lift the rifle. To point it at him.

Or for more of them to drop down and surround him.

He waited for whatever the hell to unfold; he didn't have a clue.

Only that it wasn't going to be good. He knew that much.

He watched the Liberator crouch down towards Jarrod's body —towards him—when suddenly he heard shooting above.

The Liberator turned around.

Looked up at the trap door.

And then he stood up and tried to clamber back up there.

Billy lay there, and he watched. Lay there and watched him struggle as the gunshots rang out above ground.

He lay there and...

Suddenly he felt something.

In Jarrod's pocket.

Something sharp digging into his leg.

He looked down, and he saw it sticking out of his pocket.

A knife.

He gritted his teeth. He had a chance.

A chance to protect himself.

A chance to defend himself.

A chance to take that Liberator out if he had to.

He watched the Liberator turn around.

Pace across the ground, right past him.

Towards that opening.

He watched him disappear into the darkness.

Towards whatever awaited him down there.

And he stayed still—very fucking still—until he was absolutely sure he was alone.

And when he was sure, he knew there was no more time for waiting around.

He pushed Jarrod's body away from him with all his strength, and he stood up.

He stared into the darkness. Yanked the knife away from Jarrod and held it as he looked down that opening.

He had to go down there.

He didn't have a choice.

He crouched down, and he crept slowly through this earthy tunnel. It smelled damp and rotten. And that rotten stench only got worse the further he got through this tunnel.

He kept on going, the ground getting muddier and slippier. It felt like it was getting darker too, which he found hard to believe since it was already very fucking dark.

He kept on squinting in the darkness as the gunshots and the footsteps rang out from above when suddenly he saw something ahead that made him stop in his tracks.

Light.

A way out?

It had to be.

The Liberator had got away, and Marco had got away, so it had to be.

He started to run towards it on this slippery ground, still covered in Jarrod's crusting blood when suddenly he saw something in the light.

Something that stopped him in his tracks again.

A head.

A head, sitting there.

Eyes open.

Mouth wide.

Staring up at Billy with dead eyes.

Grey skin.

Spiders crawling all over it.

Cobwebs between her teeth.

It didn't take Billy long to realise this was Jade's head.

He swallowed a sickly lump in his throat. Jarrod must've brought it here. He must've brought it here and kept it here.

Fuck. That was sad.

Sick, but sad.

He turned away from Jade and towards the light, knowing full well he had only one goal on his mind right now.

Getting the hell out of here.

He clambered up the muddy slope, towards that light, towards that exit.

Closer, and closer, and closer...

He took another step and went to open whatever door this was into the outside world when he felt something that made his stomach sink.

The trap door, or whatever it was.

It wasn't budging.

He pushed it again, a couple of times. It had to open.

Because Marco had got out.

And the Liberator had got out.

So it had to open.

Right?

Unless…

Right on cue, he heard something behind him.

Footsteps.

He froze.

Stayed still.

Like a rabbit in the headlights.

And then, sure enough, bright light illuminated the darkness.

He turned around and saw someone standing there.

Rifle in hand.

Shining a torch at him.

The Liberator.

He was still here.

CHAPTER THIRTY-THREE

Billy saw the Liberator standing there pointing his rifle at him in the darkness, and he knew he was fucked.

It was dark, but for the bright torchlight beaming straight at him. The confines of this underground lair suddenly seemed a whole lot more claustrophobic—and they weren't exactly airy to begin with. He couldn't hear footsteps or gunshots outside anymore beyond that locked hatch he was so close to escaping through. All he could hear was the racing of his heart, blood whooshing through his head.

His ears ringing after the pistol shot earlier.

And the sound of the Liberator, breathing.

The air was thick with the smell of rot, but that rot was mostly replaced by the smell of sweat now.

Billy's own sweat, he knew.

Because he always sweated when he was afraid. When he felt cornered.

And right now, he was very afraid.

Right now, he felt very cornered.

He stood there gripping Jarrod's knife, the coin-like taste of Jarrod's blood clinging to his lips.

The Liberator stood opposite him.

Rifle pointed at him.

And Billy really did feel like this was it. Like it *had* to be it.

Nobody was coming to save him.

He stood there, and he stared at the Liberator. Or rather, his darkened silhouette. He hadn't said a word. He hadn't heard *any* of these Liberators say a word.

Which, in a way, made them even more creepy.

It made them even scarier.

More... robotic, in a way.

More like the force of nature Meg described them as.

And as he stood there, awaiting his inevitable death, a new found confidence awoke inside Billy.

Like he could say anything and get away with it, 'cause what did it matter anymore?

He was going to die.

Why not try and find out a little about who these people were —if only for his own benefit, now?

"Who are you people?" Billy asked.

The Liberator didn't say a word.

He just kept his rifle pointed at Billy.

Time stretching on before him.

"Really? You're just gonna blank me? Grant me one dying wish, at least."

He didn't expect the Liberator to say a word.

Didn't expect him to say anything at all as he stood there, knife in his hand.

But then something surprising happened.

The Liberator spoke.

"We're the monsters you created."

Billy frowned. *We're the monsters you created.* What was that supposed to mean?

Whatever the hell it meant, it sent a shiver down the back of his neck.

The Liberator lifted the rifle.

He steadied it on Billy.

Went to pull the trigger.

And Billy knew it was over.

He knew he was fucked.

He waited for the bullet to pierce his throat when suddenly, a realisation dawned on him.

If the Liberator hadn't escaped...

Then Marco hadn't escaped either.

Right?

Just as the thought crept up on him, he saw a figure emerge behind the Liberator.

Marco.

He cracked the Liberator over the head with a rock.

The Liberator fell down to the ground, onto his knees.

Billy didn't hesitate.

He ran over to him.

Lifted his knife.

Went to ram it into the Liberator's chest.

And then he realised something.

In that instant, he realised something.

The Liberator.

They could use him.

They could keep him alive. Take him hostage. Find out about who he was and who his people were.

He stood there, knife in hand, time standing still.

The Liberator looked up at him as he sat there on his knees.

He opened his mouth.

Went to speak.

And then Marco cracked him over the head with the rock again.

The Liberator fell to the ground.

Twitched.

Blood spurting from his lips.

And then, nothing at all.

Nothing but stillness.

"Fuck," Billy said.

"You're welcome."

"I'm guessing now's not the time to ask if you believe me now, hmm?"

Marco shook his head. "Whatever. We—we need to get back to Eastbrook. We need to warn them. There's lots of these people. And if they're really heading there... then home's in danger. Real danger."

Which is exactly what I was fucking trying to tell you before, dipshit.

"Any ways out you've seen?" Billy asked.

"Just the opening here. But it'll take some punching. Didn't want to draw the attention of these creeps back this way."

"Out there," Billy said. "They were firing at someone. Chasing someone. I thought it was you."

Marco shrugged. "I'm still here."

Billy stood there in the darkness, and all kinds of thoughts and questions raced through his mind. Who were the Liberators chasing out there? Was it Meg?

And that thing the Liberator said to him.

We're the monsters you created.

What did that mean?

He crouched down. Looked at the Liberator. A man no older than forty. Bald head. Grey uniform. Whoever these people were, they were well drilled, well supplied, and clearly well organised.

"Either way," Billy said, "we're gonna have to get out of this place. And at least we have a tool for the job, now."

He grabbed the Liberator's rifle from his twitching fingertips.

Lifted it.

Walked over to the hatch.

"You sure that's a good idea?" Marco asked.

Billy looked back. He listened outside for any sounds but didn't hear a thing.

"I don't think we've got much choice, do you?"

Marco shook his head. "I guess not."

Billy turned around.

Pointed the rifle at the hinges between the hatch.

"Cover your ears," he said.

And then he pulled the trigger.

The hatch blew away upon gunshot.

His ears rang like mad.

"Shit," Marco shouted. "You coulda given me more of a heads up."

Billy smirked. He didn't want to tell Marco that making him suffer a little was slightly part of the plan. "Come on. We've got to get out of here."

They stepped outside the hatch into the woods. The sun had gone in, and it was raining a little. The woods *looked* quiet, and they *looked* empty. But Billy knew far better than that at this stage.

He looked back at the little underground lair he'd fallen into.

Marco looked back, too.

And he knew what he was thinking of.

Jarrod.

The man who'd put him through hell.

One of the men who'd made his childhood a misery.

Dead inside there.

And alongside him?

Another threat.

A threat from the past and a threat from the future.

"Come on," Billy said. "No looking back. Not anymore. Just forward."

Marco looked at him. Nodded. Half-smiled. "I'm sorry for doubting you."

Billy didn't expect that. "I'm sorry... I'm sorry for doubting you too. I was really fucking convinced you'd killed Jorah to set me up."

"And I was really fucking convinced *you'd* killed Jorah. But not to set me up. Just because you're batshit crazy."

"Charming."

Marco smiled back at him.

They stood together in the woods. In front of that lair of past and future demons.

And Billy took a deep breath.

He knew exactly what he had to do next.

"Back to Eastbrook," he said. "Back home. We need to warn our people. Before it's too late."

CHAPTER THIRTY-FOUR

He stood over his fallen comrade and felt a twinge of regret.

It was dark in this underground hideout, and it stunk. Stunk of rot and decay. There was a woman's decapitated head, no older than her early twenties, in the corner of this section of the hideout. It seemed to have seen some serious decomposition, so must've been in here a while—and he guessed it was responsible for the worst of the smells.

There were other smells, too. Urine. Faeces. Vomit. Body odour. Not a nice place. Not a nice place at all.

But as much as his mind was naturally trying to paint a picture of this place and what sort of inhabitants it housed, he couldn't turn his attention away from his fallen comrade.

He lay there, bleeding from his cracked skull. There was a rock beside him, covered in blood. His rifle was gone.

Which irked him somewhat.

He was supposed to be careful. All of them were supposed to be careful.

He'd acted rash by coming down here alone.

He'd got himself killed—and had one of their weapons stolen.

And that was not good.

That was not good at all.

He heard footsteps approaching. Saw two more of his comrades standing over the body.

"Should we bury him?" one of them asked.

He looked down at the body of his fallen comrade, and instead of feeling pity, instead of feeling sympathy, he felt anger.

Because he'd let the scum get away.

Nobody ever let the scum get away and got away with it themselves.

"There's no time," he said.

"Are you sure? It won't take—"

"You know your orders," he barked. "All of us do."

His comrades looked back at him. Glassy-eyed. No emotion.

Just straight stares right into his eyes.

"We've waited too long," he said. "We can't risk them reaching our next target and warning them. Any resistance is a failure."

"Then what do we do next?"

He turned around and looked out at the grey skies. At the falling rain. At the beautiful trees and the glorious, perfect world outside... and he thought about just how much more perfect it was going to be when it was cleansed of its greatest toxic.

"We escalate our operation to the next stage," he said. "We follow our orders. We gather our troops. And we launch our attack. Now."

CHAPTER THIRTY-FIVE

Walking through the woods as fast as they could, Billy and Marco didn't say much to each other.

Thick clouds blotted out the sun above. It was still. Very still. Sounded cliche, but it really did feel like the proverbial calm before the storm.

He just hoped that storm wasn't as imminent as it felt.

He looked at Marco, who walked alongside him. Marco had barely even looked at him since their escape from Jarrod's underground lair. Just kept his head down and walked on.

And Billy got it. He appreciated the urgency.

But at the same time... it felt like a pandora's box had been opened where Marco was concerned.

The truth about his past.

The truth about what he'd been through, at the hands of Ramiro, at the hands of Jarrod.

The truth about the pair of them that Billy hadn't seen in front of him, staring him in the eyes: he and Marco weren't so different after all.

"You okay?" Billy asked.

Marco glanced around at him. Frowned. "Sure."

Billy nodded. He wanted to just accept Marco's reassurance. After all, he didn't exactly want to engage himself in a deep conversation with this guy. Not now. The fate of Eastbrook was in their hands. Now really wasn't the time.

But at the same time... Billy just felt like there were things between them that needed to be acknowledged.

Stones he couldn't leave unturned.

"I know... I know what it feels like. When you get revenge."

Marco looked around at him. His eyes narrowed even more. The look on his face screamed at Billy to back off. Not to go there.

But Billy was already there. And there was no turning back.

"I know that feeling of... of strength, at first. Of relief. And then... and then there's an emptiness. Because you realise the thing you've been trying to get revenge on for so long is... is gone. And there's nothing in its place. But then it gets worse than that. Because... because the anger is still there. The pain is still there. And getting revenge does nothing to change that."

Marco stared at him in the silence of the woods. The only sounds were from the birds above, chirping in the trees. No breeze. No footsteps. Nothing.

"I... I'm sorry for what you went through. For what we both went through. I'm sorry it... I'm sorry it drove you to hate me. Because I know now. I understand. I get it. You saw yourself in me. Seeing me was like... like looking in a mirror and being reminded of a past you desperately wanted to let go of. But we can't let go. We'll live with it forever. We just... we just have to learn how to grow around it, I guess. So it doesn't define us. So it doesn't swallow us whole."

Marco stared at him. Still hadn't said a word. Which was slightly disconcerting 'cause it meant his reaction could go one of two ways.

"I know it looked like I killed Jorah—"

"I know you didn't kill Jorah."

"Marco, I get that now. But I mean—"

"I've always known you didn't kill Jorah."

Billy narrowed his eyes. "What?"

And then a coldness set in.

Was this an admission?

Was this a confession?

After all this time, was he finally—

"I saw someone else, too," Marco said. "Standing outside your house in the dark. And then again, when you ran away. I saw them. I just... I don't know. I was so sure it was you. I was so desperate *for* it to be you. And the way everything fell into place so neatly. Especially after what happened three months ago. I dunno. I guess I just... I just wanted it to be true."

Okay. So he wasn't confessing. Which was fortunate because Billy really didn't fucking fancy being stuck alone in the middle of the woods with Jorah's killer right now.

"It made more sense for it to be you," Marco said. "Especially..."

He stopped. Looked at the ground. Shook his head.

"Especially what?"

"I saw who it was, okay?"

Billy narrowed his eyes. "You saw... What are you talking about?"

"I should've been more... more up front about it, I dunno. But it didn't make sense. Not in the way it makes sense with you."

"I don't know what you're talking about."

"I wanted you to go down for it. You're right. And a part of me will never be able to look you in the eyes without remembering what that sick cunt did to me. The horrible things they all did to us."

The garage.

The darkness of the garage looming again.

"But you know where you're wrong?"

Billy shrugged.

"I *do* feel better knowing that cunt is dead. My only regret is I couldn't make him suffer more for what he did."

They stood there in the woods. A little breeze picking up now. Specks of rain falling down heavier.

But as Billy stood there in the woods opposite Marco, there was only one thing on his mind.

"Who did you think you saw?" Billy asked.

Marco shook his head. "It still doesn't make sense to me. I still don't understand. Still can't figure it out—"

"Marco," Billy said. "Who did you see?"

Marco stared right into Billy's eyes for the first time in... well, the first time *ever*? Probably.

He shook his head.

"You're not going to believe this," he said. "And I know it doesn't really make sense. But I saw... I saw Faye."

CHAPTER THIRTY-SIX

Faye stared out into the woods and couldn't understand how things had gone so wrong, so quickly.

It was morning. The birds were singing. She usually loved the sound of birdsong. But today, it was just noise. Like nails on a chalkboard, right beside her.

Reminding her of what had happened.

She looked out at the trees. Looked at their dark, alien silhouettes against the bright sky. And as she sat there, she couldn't believe how empty she felt. She couldn't believe that she missed Connor as much as she did.

Because he wasn't good to her.

He was downright awful with her.

But at the same time... she missed him.

And she hated how empty everything made her feel.

She looked out at the trees and remembered walking out there one night. Clearing her head in the quiet nighttime air. The smell of the trees. The cold grass between her toes.

And that certainty in her mind.

A terrifying certainty that she'd never experienced before.

A certainty about killing herself.

She wanted to end her life. She wanted to end the pain.

She wanted to stop suffering.

And as far as she was concerned, there was only one way.

She remembered reaching a tree and staring up at it and wondering if she could wrap something around that branch when she heard movement.

At first, she was afraid. Because she knew there were bad people outside. And she knew she'd wandered a little far from home at an hour that wasn't exactly the safest.

But then, when she'd seen the man standing opposite her, in a way, she'd felt a sense of relief.

Because maybe she wouldn't have to kill herself.

Maybe someone would do the trick for her, and then it would all be over without her involvement.

But things... hadn't gone that way.

They'd gone very, very differently.

She walked away from the window. Back into the bedroom. Her heart raced. Her jaw tightened up. She'd ground her teeth down more in the last few days than she had her whole life—and she was already a tooth-grinder.

She didn't want to think about what'd happened.

What'd driven her to do it.

Because it didn't even *feel* like her.

But what that man in the woods promised her.

The future he'd promised her.

And the future he'd *showed* her.

She hated to admit it, but it eclipsed anything Eastbrook had to offer her.

She climbed into bed. Lay there and stared at the blank ceiling. Waited for morning to arrive. She wondered where Billy was. She'd heard the shouting outside. She'd *seen* him outside.

He was so close to catching her.

She wondered how things might've gone if he had.

Just like he was so close to finding her walking out of Jorah's house that morning, too.

She felt bad. Because she knew how this looked for Billy. And she liked Billy; she really did.

But the future they offered her.

The future they decided she was going to be a part of.

That mattered more than anything else.

She closed her eyes, and she saw it flash before her.

The blood.

Jorah's terrified eyes staring up at her.

Confused.

Confused as she buried the blade into his stomach.

Again.

Again.

Again.

Just as the man in the woods told her to.

She remembered apologising to him.

She remembered whispering to him that she didn't really understand herself, but it was for a better future.

She remembered seeing her blood-splattered hands in the mirror as she left his bedroom, and for a moment, she felt total horror.

What was she?

Who had she become?

She swallowed a lump in her throat.

Pushed those memories to one side.

And she focused on the one thing she could cling to.

The one thing keeping her going.

And that was the better future.

The better future that was on its way.

The better future she'd been promised.

The better future that was going to arrive.

Today.

CHAPTER THIRTY-SEVEN

"Faye?" Billy said.

Marco nodded. "I know. It doesn't make any sense."

Billy shook his head. Stood there in the woods with Marco. The sky growing even cloudier by the second. Rain falling down heavier from above. Total silence. Total silence hanging in the air, especially after Marco's claim. A sickly taste creeping up into his mouth.

"Faye?" Billy said.

Marco lowered his head. "I know it doesn't add up."

"Are we talking about the same Faye here?"

"There's only one Faye," Marco said.

Billy shook his head. Faye? It didn't make sense. Was he seriously suggesting she'd killed Jorah?

That she'd brutalised him like that?

No. It didn't make any sense. It just didn't add up.

"You can't be serious, can you?"

"I'm only telling you what I saw," Marco said. "I saw her outside your house. I wasn't sure it was her. It was... it was too dark, y'know? And I... I saw her in the streets just after you did a runner, too. I saw her peeking around a damned corner in the dead of night. I've no idea what she was doing there at that time. But it was definitely her."

Billy shook his head. Faye. No. It couldn't be Faye. She couldn't be the traitor.

It just didn't make sense.

"I didn't want to think she might be involved somehow. Just one of those things you bury, you know? And I didn't think about it. Not really. I was still dead certain you were responsible. But then... finding out about these people. And hearing what you said about this all being a setup. About some kind of traitor. Some kind of betrayal. It's... I dunno, Billy. But I feel like it sorta makes sense."

Billy still couldn't speak. Still couldn't say a word. Just stood there, shaking his head.

He couldn't deny the feelings he felt for Faye. The crush he had on her.

That deep sense that maybe someday, there could be something between them.

He knew it was stupid. Fairytale shit. Childish, immature crap that he really shouldn't be thinking about right now.

But at the same time... he felt this deep sense of disappointment weighing down on his shoulders.

It couldn't be Faye.

He simply couldn't believe it.

He took a deep breath then. Tried to push the thought to one side. Because ultimately, right now, it didn't matter.

Right now, it was secondary to his main goal.

Getting back to Eastbrook.

Warning them before the Liberators arrived.

"We keep going," Billy said. "We can worry about who did or didn't kill Jorah later. Right now... right now, this is what matters."

He walked. Saw Marco following him with his gaze. Not saying a word.

He powered through the woods. He had no idea how far from home he was, only that he felt like he was getting closer.

And as much as he tried to focus on the road ahead, as much as he tried to keep his attention completely singular... he just couldn't stop thinking about the thought that Faye might have something to do with this entire mess.

No. Marco had this wrong.

It couldn't be her.

It wasn't possible.

He walked further through the woods. His legs aching. His head spinning. And the pain in his hands growing more and more intense.

The urgency growing.

Thoughts circling his mind.

What if the Liberators were already there?

He gritted his teeth. Shook his head. No point mulling it over. No point dwelling on it.

Just had to get back home.

Had to keep walking and had to get back home.

Had to pray.

He walked further through the endless maze of trees when suddenly he saw something in front of him.

Something he recognised.

Aoife's tree.

Which meant he was almost there.

They were almost back.

"Come on," Billy said. "We're... we're almost back."

Heart beating faster.

Sweat pouring down his face.

Shaking.

Shaking with adrenaline.

Shaking with anticipation.

He ran up the slope. Ran up through the trees. Eastbrook would be in view soon.

He'd see what state it was in.

See whether it was in flames.

Smell the smoke.

Hear the gunshots and the screams...

He clambered up the slope, and he thought of Steve.

He thought of Rex.

And... he thought of Faye.

It couldn't be her.

She couldn't be involved.

Right?

He reached the top of the slope, and he braced himself for the worst as he looked down at Eastbrook.

There was no smoke.

There was no fire.

There were no gunshots.

No screaming.

It was just Eastbrook.

Eastbrook, as he knew it.

As he'd *always* known it.

Relief washed over him. But that relief was tinged with an even greater urgency.

"We've got to get back," Billy said. "We've—we've got to warn them. Before it's too late."

Marco nodded. "You can say that again."

They ran down the slope towards the gates of Eastbrook.

And he felt nervous. Really fucking nervous about the prospect of going back there.

Because Marco might know the truth, but nobody else did.

They might shoot him on sight.

They might throw him in the cells.

He might not get a chance to say his piece.

He ran down the slope. Saw the guards standing atop the fence, guns in hand.

And he held on to his rifle, too. The one he'd grabbed from the Liberator.

He held it close to his chest.

Because he had to be ready for the Liberators.

He had to be ready for them.

Just in case.

Just—

"Stop!"

A voice.

A voice from right in front of him.

The guards.

Standing there.

Rifles pointed down at him.

"You need to open the gates," Billy shouted.

"Drop your weapon and get down on the ground."

Billy shook his head. He dropped the rifle. And he got right down on the ground. Because it didn't matter that he was doing what they told him. He just had to convince them to hear him out.

"Both of you!"

"What?" Marco said.

"On the ground. Right now!"

Marco looked at Billy, shrugged, and shook his head.

And he got down on the ground, next to Billy.

The pair of them lay there on the ground. Billy looked up at the gate in front of him. Saw people there now. Members of the community peering round the corner. Guards, weapons raised, heading his way. He didn't know how this would go. But he had to try. He had to try his fucking best here, or it was game over. It was time up.

He couldn't just lie here and wait for them to throw him in a cell.

Or worse.

"There's someone coming," Billy shouted.

Silence in response.

"There's—there's someone out there. Someone dangerous. And they're heading right here. And I know... I know you don't want to listen to me right now. I know you think I'm responsible for what happened to Jorah. But that's—that's what they want you to think."

"Stay on the ground and don't move a muscle," one of the guards shouted.

"Someone... someone betrayed us," Billy said. Stopping short of accusing Faye. Because he still couldn't believe it. Still didn't want to accept it. "I met someone. Out in the woods. Meg, she's called. She... she told me about what these people did to her communities. And I've seen these people for myself. I've seen the looks in their eyes. I've seen how well equipped they are. And... and we won't have a chance. Not unless we—not unless we flee Eastbrook. Not unless we regroup and—and grow stronger. Stand together with other communities. Not unless we fight."

The guards' footsteps grew nearer.

Their guns still pointed at Billy.

At Marco.

Clock ticking.

Time running out.

"We need to be ready," Billy said. "Because if we aren't... it's the end of everything."

The guards, led by Sergeant Kirk, walked up to Billy's rifle. Kicked it away.

And then they looked down at him.

Looked down at Marco.

Rifles in their hands.

"Please," Billy said. "You need to listen to us. To both of us. You need to hear us out. Marco?"

Marco looked up at Sergeant Kirk, and he nodded. "Much as

it pains me to admit it, Billy's right. He's right about everything. I've seen these people. Unless we do something—fast—we can say goodnight to Eastbrook."

Billy looked around at Kirk again.

Waited for him to say something.

Waited for him to realise they weren't bullshitting here and to accept there was more to this than first thought.

And then, finally, he spoke.

"That's a nice story," Kirk said. "If we didn't already have a witness statement. About the pair of you."

Billy frowned. "A witness statement? What—"

"Someone stepped forward. Said they saw the pair of you together when Billy did a runner. Said they saw you spending an awful lot of time together lately. And saw you leaving Jorah's house together, too."

Marco shook his head. "That's—that's bullshit."

"I don't care what you have to say right now. These are dangerous times. And the rest of the council are using our privileges to strip you of yours."

"Bullshit," Marco said. "You're playing into their hands. Don't you see?"

"I'm arresting you both on suspicion of the murder of Jorah. You can moan about it as much as you want. But the community has spoken. Eastbrook has spoken."

Billy looked up into Kirk's eyes, and he saw the terrifying look of a man who'd already made his mind up.

He looked up, and he saw the terrifying eyes of a *community* that'd already made its mind up.

He felt hands grab him.

Felt guards drag him to his feet.

Heard Marco kicking and trying to break free, pleading his innocence.

And as the guards dragged the pair of them back into the

walls of Eastbrook, Billy saw something that made his body turn cold.

Faye stood right by the gates.

Staring at him with wide eyes that told him everything he needed to know.

Guilty eyes.

CHAPTER THIRTY-EIGHT

Billy sat in the darkness of his cell and tried not to think about the garage.

But in trying not to think about the garage, much like trying not to think of that proverbial motherfucking pink elephant, what did Billy think about?

Yeah. The goddamned garage.

He sat against the cold brick wall of the cell. Ahead of him, darkness, but for a little window of light in the door. The old cells in the police station. Freezing as hell... or, well, not hell. The opposite of hell. Heaven? Fuck if he knew what the temperature was like in the afterlife.

And what did it matter?

He was cold. Shivering. Although, okay, part of that shaking might just be nerves.

Nerves about the fact he was stuck in this cell, and it reminded him of the garage he'd been locked away in as a kid.

Nerves about the thought that Jorah's murder was being pinned on him.

And mostly, nerves about the imminent plight of Eastbrook.

The approaching forces of the Liberators.

Who he knew for a fact were getting closer, and closer, and closer.

He sat back against the wall. His head ached. His throat was dry, and he could really do with some frigging water right now.

He could hear things outside. Muffled footsteps and distant voices. He wanted to shout out to them. To tell them to come to his cell. That time was running out, and he needed to speak to them. He needed to warn them.

But he'd tried all that already.

His throat was sore from trying.

He sat there, and he closed his burning eyes, and he thought about Faye. The look in her eyes. She'd betrayed them, no doubt about it. Still couldn't believe it. Still couldn't accept it. Still couldn't understand it.

But for some reason—whether she'd been promised something greater than this or whatever—she'd stabbed the entire community in the back.

And now Eastbrook was staring down the barrel of a gun.

And there was nothing Billy could do about it.

He stayed there, staring into the darkness behind his closed eyes. He smelled the damp clinging to the walls. Tasted it, all stagnant and rotten on his lips.

He felt the cold fingertips against his spine.

Heard the gruff laughter of one of those fuckers who'd hurt him.

And he froze.

Froze to the spot.

Caught in fear, all over again.

But this time, as he sat here, he felt something different.

Something different entirely.

A sense of inevitability.

A sense that, of course, his life had come to this.

Of course, everything had built up to this moment.

He was meant to be locked away in a cell in the darkness.

That was what his life came to.

It was the place he always returned to—whether in his waking life or in his nightmares.

And it wasn't going to leave him alone.

He stood up. Walked over to the cell door.

He banged his sore, burning knuckles against it.

Banged, and banged, and banged.

Because that fear inside was building up again.

That fear about Steve.

About Rex.

About all the people here he cared about.

And how he couldn't just let the Liberators step in here and wipe out his community.

"You have to listen to me!" Billy shouted, his voice cracking, all croaky and sore. "You—you have to listen to me. I know you think I'm crazy, but your lives depend on it!"

No response.

Just his own voice, echoing against the cell walls.

"Leave me here if you have to," Billy said. "But just... just get yourselves away from here. Please. You've no idea what's coming. You've no idea what's coming."

He heard his own breaking voice again as he stared at the cell door ahead of him, and he stopped.

He stepped back.

Walked away from the door.

Over to the back of the cell.

He sat down against the cold brick wall.

Lay his head back.

"You've no idea what's coming," he muttered.

And all the time, as he sat there, defeated, those words the Liberator said to him kept on swirling around his mind.

We're the monsters you created.

CHAPTER THIRTY-NINE

Billy knew something was wrong the moment he heard the bang.

He spun around. Looked into the darkness, over at the cell door. The hairs on the back of his neck stood on end. 'Cause that bang was loud. So loud it'd rocked the cells. Made the walls shake.

And as he stared over at the little light shining through the grating on the cell door, he felt a sense of dread completely fill his chest.

Anxiety filling him from head to toe like someone had turned on a tap and started filling his body with it.

Because he knew what that bang meant.

He'd tried to deny it. He'd tried to convince himself that maybe he *was* just losing his mind. That maybe it *was* an exaggeration. And that maybe he was exactly where he needed to be—locked away in a cell in the darkness.

But hearing that bang.

Hearing that explosion.

His heart started thumping.

The butterflies in his stomach multiplied, duplicated.

He felt so anxious he could barely breathe. Like a vice grip was tightening around his chest and getting tighter and tighter and tighter...

But he couldn't afford to lose his shit right now.

He had to stay present.

And he had to face up to the horrifying truth.

The Liberators were here.

He got up. Walked across his cell, over to the cell door. He banged against it. Hard.

No response.

Nothing but echoes.

He stood there in the dark, and he thought of that explosion. He thought about Steve. He thought about Rex.

He thought about the stories Meg told him about her communities and how they fell.

And he thought about his community.

His home.

He'd tried to stop this.

He'd tried to warn them.

And now...

He went to bang against the cell door again when he heard something else that made his fear even worse.

Gunshots.

Screams.

He heard those gunshots, and he heard those screams, and instinctively, he closed his eyes.

Squeezed his burning, stinging eyes shut.

Because as much as there wasn't any doubt about it, that was the confirmation he needed.

The Liberators were *definitely* fucking here.

And he was trapped in a cell, unable to do a thing about it.

He banged against the cell door again. Shaking. "Hey! Let me out!"

But his voice just disappeared into the silence.

His banging went unnoticed.

"Let me the fuck out!"

He banged against the cell door some more before kicking it and stepping back. Fuck. This was bad. This was really fucking bad. He needed to be out there. He needed to be helping his people. Steve. Rex. So many people he cared about.

He couldn't just stand around in here while the Liberators launched their assault outside.

He couldn't just stand around here while his people died.

He looked around the darkness of his cell. Looked for a crack in the walls. Looked for a way through the tiny barred window.

He looked at the cell door and at that small bit of grating, which a minuscule bit of light shone in through.

He looked everywhere for an exit, for an escape route, for any kind of way out.

But there was nothing.

This was a fucking cell, after all.

He stood in the middle of the darkness, and he'd never felt as useless in his life before.

He'd never felt as trapped in his life before.

And he'd never felt as scared in his life bef...

No.

No, that wasn't true.

The garage.

The garage as a kid.

The cold air.

The stench of sweat.

And the man standing in front of him, smirk on his face.

No. No, don't go there. Get away from there, now.

But as much as he tried to breathe deeply, he couldn't push the memory from his mind.

As much as he tried to force those thoughts away... it just got worse.

The darkness grew darker.

The stench of sweat, piss, and shit grew more disgusting.

The coppery taste of blood at the back of his throat grew stronger.

Not now, not now, not now...

He felt the fingers touch his skin.

He felt them stroking his neck.

He felt himself disappearing into that same void he used to go back then, back when he was a child.

That same empty void.

The place where he could protect himself.

The place where he didn't feel any pain.

Don't go there now.

You need to stay here.

You need to stay here, and you need to get out of this cell, and you need to fight—

"It's time you fought something else first, Billy," a voice said.

Right in front of him, he saw somebody standing there.

Ramiro.

Ramiro, just as he remembered him.

That same smirk on his face.

That same smell of aftershave doing nothing to mask the sour stench of his breath.

And that same look in his eyes.

"It's about time you fought your past," he said. "About time you faced up to some of the things you've done."

"Once and for all," another voice said.

This voice made the hairs on Billy's arms stand right on end.

Made him freeze right on the spot.

But he turned around.

He turned around slowly, and he saw him standing there in the darkness.

He saw the man standing over him.

He saw the familiar brown eyes.

And the smile that looked even more like his than he realised.

He saw the belt around his knuckles.
And he saw Mum's decapitated head stuffed under his arm.
The one he'd been trying to run from.
The one he'd been trying to hide from.
For so, so many years, the truth he'd tried to escape.
"Hello, Billy," Dad said. "Long time no see."

CHAPTER FORTY

"You look surprised to see me, son. Were you expecting that day in the church to be the last? Really?"

Billy stood in the middle of the darkness. The cell around him had vanished and was replaced by the familiar garage walls.

Only...

No.

The walls were changing,

They were changing into somewhere different entirely.

But somewhere else familiar.

He looked at the walls and saw cream wallpaper appearing.

The cartoon elephants and the lions standing there on the paper, with little smiles on their faces.

Oh no.

Oh God, no.

He couldn't go *here*.

Anywhere but *here*.

He squeezed his eyes shut. This wasn't real. This was all in his head. It was all in his head, and he needed to snap out of it. He needed to wake up from it.

And then he heard those words echoing in his ears.

"Just because you're not really here now doesn't mean it's not real."

He sighed. Because those words were true.

Spoken by Dad.

Completely true.

He stood there, shaking with adrenaline. His stomach knotting. A pain there like he'd been punched.

And he knew he couldn't run from the truth anymore.

He knew he needed to face up to the truth.

Once and for all.

He opened his eyes.

He was in his childhood bedroom. It was just like he remembered it. That animal wallpaper. The little television sitting there at the foot of his bed. His dark, wooden wardrobes.

And the door.

The door, with the light shining through it.

And standing in front of that door, Billy saw Dad.

Billy was in bed now. Under the covers. Frozen solid. Even though he could see, he knew his eyes were closed.

Just like he used to keep them closed as a kid.

Pretend you're asleep. Just pretend you're asleep...

He heard Dad's footsteps creaking across the bedroom floor, and dread built up inside him.

Footsteps creaking closer.

And closer.

His heart started racing. Breathing grew difficult.

Keep it together, Billy. Keep it together.

Don't let him know you're awake.

Don't let him know...

Then he felt it.

The cold fingers on his skin.

Making his muscles tighten.

Making his body seize up.

The smell of alcohol.

And the darkness.

The darkness behind his closed eyes.

Only...

He wasn't in the garage.

He knew he wasn't in the garage.

He was somewhere else.

Somewhere much more familiar.

Somewhere he'd tried to deny any wrongdoing ever went down for his entire life.

He felt Dad's fingers stroking his skin.

And instead of letting it happen, instead of letting it just unfold, because he was always too afraid to do anything different than just let it unfold... Billy opened his eyes.

Dad stood over him.

Staring down at him. Sweat pouring down his face.

Tears raining down from his eyes.

He saw Dad standing over him, and he wanted to close his eyes.

He wanted to revert to his shell again.

Or hide in that place he'd learned to hide inside for so many years already.

But this time... he knew he couldn't go back inside that place.

This time... he knew he had to face up to Dad.

He knew he couldn't run from him anymore.

"I didn't expect you to open your eyes," Dad said. His voice echoing, floating all around him. "I expected you to keep them shut. Just like you always kept them shut. Just like you always have..."

No. Don't face it. Don't accept it. Fight it. Fight it because it didn't happen like you think it happened. Fight it because it was different to how you remember. Fight it because—

"I appreciate you choosing not to remember," Dad said. Stroking Billy's bare arm with those icy cold hands. "Or rather...

to remember things differently to how they actually happened. To how they actually went down.

Don't go there, don't go there, don't—

"But you see the truth now," Dad said. "You remember it. And you can't fight it anymore. Can you?"

He looked up into Dad's eyes, and he wanted to keep running.

He wanted to keep fighting.

He wanted to keep hiding.

But now, lying here, he knew the days of running and hiding from the truth were behind him.

Way behind him.

"You abused me," Billy said.

Dad's face didn't change. His expression didn't change.

He just kept on stroking Billy's arm. Again, and again, and again.

"You abused me like... like Ramiro's people did. But it... it was worse from you. Because I thought you were my dad. Even though... even though you told me I wasn't your son. I thought you were... I thought you were my dad. And even after you did those horrible things... I still loved you. I still wanted to love you."

Dad's expression didn't change.

He just kept on stroking Billy's arm.

Mechanically.

Again and again.

"And I've even felt guilty. For killing you. For killing you so... so easily. But now I don't feel guilty. Now, I wish I could do it again. Only... only worse. Because... because I'm not going to run from you anymore. I'm going to accept what you did to me."

He tried to stand.

Tried to get to his feet.

But Dad's hands just pinned Billy down.

The more he tried to stand, the harder he seemed to press him.

And that made Billy feel anxious.

That made Billy feel afraid.

You don't have to be anxious anymore.

You don't have to be afraid anymore.

"I'm going to accept what you did to me. And... and I'm going to accept that I didn't deserve it. I didn't deserve what you did. I didn't deserve what *anyone* did. I didn't deserve the pain. I didn't deserve the pain I caused myself to try to make myself forget. Because... because I need to feel it. I need to feel it. Or I'll never grow through it."

Dad smiled. Started laughing. "You'll *never* grow through it, Billy. It will always be with you."

But Billy shook his head.

He took a deep breath.

"I *will* grow through it. Because you aren't my dad. You never were a dad to me. Steve is my dad. And he needs me now. The community needs me now."

He closed his eyes, and he took a deep breath, and he felt the pain and the sadness and the trauma inside.

And then he let out a cry.

He pushed himself up.

Up, against his heavy grip.

Up, against all his strength.

I am strong.

Pushed, even though he pressed him down even harder.

Pushed, even though his grip got stronger and tighter.

Pushed, even though the memories, and the pain, and the fear, all got worse and worse and...

I am strong.

He let out another cry and felt the thoughts rising out of his body, bursting out of his soul.

And then he felt a weight lift from his chest.

A weight lift from his entire body.

He lay there. Totally exhausted. Head aching. Ears ringing.

And he wasn't in bed anymore.

He was... on the floor somewhere.

Somewhere cold.

He opened his eyes, and he saw the cell walls around him.

He heard the gunshots outside.

The crying outside.

The explosions and the screaming outside.

And even though he was terrified about the plight of his people, even though he was terrified about what was happening to Eastbrook... deep inside, Billy felt a sense of peace.

A sense of peace he hadn't felt for a long, long time.

He was going to be okay.

Everything was going to be okay.

He took a deep breath, closed his eyes, and felt himself slipping away into unconsciousness.

CHAPTER FORTY-ONE

Steve ran down the street as gunshots echoed behind him, and he only had one damned direction in mind.

The cells where Billy was being kept.

He ran as fast as his creaky old legs would go. Behind, he heard gunshots. So many damned gunshots.

And with gunshots, he heard screaming too.

The horrifying cries of his people.

Men.

Women.

Little'uns.

Eastbrook was under attack.

It was under attack, and unless he got to the cells and got Billy out of there, he was gonna die in those walls.

And he couldn't let that happen to his son.

To his boy.

He clenched his fists together and ran down the road. He felt frigging awful for running away from the rest of his people in their time of need. 'Cause if there was one thing Eastbrook needed right now, it was to stand together. Only chance it had of standing up to these... well, whoever the hell they were.

But at the same time, he looked around, and he saw signs that it was already too late.

The flames and the smoke rising in the distance.

Those shouts and those screams.

The bodies lying along the road.

It was already chaos here.

It was too late to put up any kind of defence.

It was about survival now.

He panted as he ran down the street. These creaky knees were way too old for running now. He was out of breath. Really dizzy. Felt like he was on the verge of just passing out.

But he had to keep his shit together.

Especially when he turned the corner and saw the police station ahead.

He stood there, hands on his knees. And he felt so frigging bad for letting Billy get locked up for murdering Jorah.

But what was he supposed to think?

Everything pointed towards it.

Maybe him being locked up was for his own good.

But now... hell, he couldn't think about any of that crap now.

He needed to get the boy out of there.

He'd let him down enough as it was.

He had to get him out.

He started to jog towards the police station when suddenly he saw something ahead that made his skin crawl.

More of those invaders.

Walking through the street but from the south this time.

Shit. They'd surrounded the place.

They'd surrounded the place, and they were walking through it and destroying every inch of it.

He saw them approaching, and he saw the police station, and he saw a small window of opportunity.

A small chance.

A chance he knew damn well he had to take.

He took a deep breath, and as much as he had no faith at all in these legs of his, he knew this might be the most important damned jog of his entire frigging life.

"Come on," Steve muttered. "You've got this."

He ran.

Ran across the street.

Knees aching.

Feet sore.

The constant echo of gunfire and cries the soundtrack to every step.

He gritted his teeth, and he focused on that police station door, and he tried not to think about the people running his way.

He tried not to think about the fact this place was surrounded.

Completely fucking surrounded.

He tried not to think about all the horrors going down.

He just had to get to the cells.

He just had to get to Billy.

He just had to—

Something whooshed past him.

So close it almost hit him.

He stopped.

Stopped dead in his tracks.

Even though he knew that was most definitely the worst thing to do right now.

They were firing at him.

They were firing at him, and if he wasn't careful, he was gonna get...

It was right on cue that he felt it.

The splitting pain, right in his right side.

He yelped. Staggered forward.

Instinctively reached for the pain.

When he lifted his hand, he saw something that made him turn cold.

Blood.

He was shot.

He was damned shot.

He looked at the enemy approaching. Saw their guns raised.

And he knew he was in danger now.

Serious frigging danger.

No more time for dallying around.

He had to get to the cells.

He started running again, although running hurt like mad. Stabbing, shooting pains split right through his body, crept up his entire right side.

You can do this, Steve. You've got this. You've got this.

He limped towards the steps, and he felt another pain.

A splitting pain, this time in his right knee.

"Argh!"

He tumbled forward.

Lying down now.

Bleeding out.

Shit.

This was it.

This was how it ended for him.

This was how he was gonna die.

On the steps of the police station.

So close to saving Billy.

So close to saving his son.

But so fucking far away, all over again.

"No!" Steve shouted.

He dragged himself up the steps towards the police station.

He just had to get inside.

Get inside without getting hit again.

'Cause as much as he knew his time was almost definitely up... he still had a chance.

He still had a chance to help Billy.

To save his boy.

One more hit, and he was pretty sure he wasn't gonna get that chance again.

He dragged himself through the door of the police station. Pushing it was hard.

But he stepped inside, and he saw those figures walking through the streets.

No urgency to them.

Just walking.

Rifles raised.

Shooting anything in sight.

He slammed the police station doors shut, and he rested his hands against the cold wood.

"Shit," he muttered. The pain in his right side and his right leg were so fucking intense, he thought he might just pass out on the spot.

But he couldn't pass out.

Not now.

He turned around and he hobbled past the reception desk.

He limped over towards the holding cells.

He just had to get to them.

He just had to get to Billy.

He just had to…

He reached the first of the cell doors, and suddenly, a sickening sense of dread surrounded him.

The cell doors.

They were locked.

Of *course* they were frigging locked.

"I'm here, Billy," Steve muttered. "I'm… I'm here. Just need to get the keys. Just need to…"

He turned around, stumbled back towards the reception.

Searched the drawers by the dusty old computers.

Searched everywhere for the keys.

But he couldn't find them.

He couldn't find them at all.

He heard something, then.

Gunshots.

Right outside.

Right in the streets outside.

Close to the police station.

So damned close.

"Come on," Steve muttered. "Got to be here somewhere. Got to be..."

He saw something, then.

Right under the desk.

A bundle of keys.

"Got 'em," he said, spinning around and turning back towards the cells. "Come on, Steve. You can do this. You're almost there. You're..."

That's when he heard it.

Heard something that made his skin turn cold.

The police station doors creaked open.

Someone was here.

CHAPTER FORTY-TWO

Billy opened his eyes.

For a moment, he felt peace. Total peace. A peace he hadn't experienced for as long as he could remember. He wanted to lie here in this weightless void. He wanted to stay here for the rest of his days.

The place where he was free of the shame.

Where he was free of the feeling that *he* was the one in the wrong.

The place where he was free of the man he used to call "Dad."

And then he heard the gunshots outside, and he remembered exactly what was going on out there.

Fear.

A bolt of fear shot right through his chest.

The Liberators.

They were in Eastbrook.

They were destroying his home.

He jolted upright. Still trapped in the darkness of his cell. The door still closed. No way out.

He took deep, shaking breaths. Sat there, totally still.

He needed to get out of this place.

He needed to get away from here.

He stood up. Walked over towards the cell door.

Pushed it.

Punched it.

And his stomach sank.

It was still locked. Of course it was still locked.

He wasn't getting out of here any time soon.

But weirdly, now, he felt something else.

A sense of peace.

A strange sense of peace about his predicament.

A certainty.

Confidence.

Confidence that the people he cared about were going to be okay.

With or without him, they were going to be okay.

He walked over to the cell window. Stood on his tiptoes. Still clung onto this hope that maybe, just maybe, he'd find a weakness in the cell. That he'd find a way out of here.

Then he shook his head.

He wasn't getting out of this cell.

He wasn't getting out of here.

He closed his burning eyes and leaned back against the wall, and he heard something.

Movement.

Footsteps outside the cell.

Someone was out there.

He opened his eyes.

Heard those footsteps getting closer.

And closer.

And then, they stopped.

He sat there. Stared over at the door.

And he waited.

He had no idea how long he sat there. No idea how long he waited.

But the longer he waited, the more convinced he became that maybe the locks were working in his favour after all.

He was locked inside.

Locked away from the Liberators.

And that made him smile.

It meant they weren't going to get to him.

It meant that no matter how hellbent on destruction they may be, they weren't getting in here any time soon.

He sat there, and he stared over at the door when suddenly, he heard something else.

Something that filled him with fear.

The sound of a lock clicking.

The sound of keys rattling.

He sat there, totally still. Nowhere to hide. And he waited.

Waited for whoever was out there to step in.

And a part of him felt hopeful. Just a small part of him.

Hopeful that maybe it was one of his people.

Maybe it was Kirk.

Maybe he was finally setting him free.

And then the cell door opened.

He held his breath.

Waited.

And when he saw who was standing there, right at the cell door, his entire world collapsed.

Steve.

Only Steve wasn't alone.

He was bleeding. Badly. From his body and his leg. He looked like he'd been beaten.

The man behind him pushed him to the floor, hard.

Cracking his head against the solid tiles.

And then he stepped inside.

Grey uniform.
Rifle in hand.
And a dead look in his eyes.
"Hello, there," the Liberator said. "What're you doing hiding away in here?"

CHAPTER FORTY-THREE

Billy saw Steve on his knees, the Liberator standing behind him with a rifle to his head, and he had to admit he felt pretty fucked right now.

Steve knelt on the cracked tiled floor of the cell right in front of the Liberator and right in front of Billy. He looked beaten and bruised. Big purple bags under his eyes. Cuts and scratches all over his face. His shirt looked a little torn, as did his jeans.

He wasn't in a good state.

And neither was Billy because of the man standing behind Steve.

He was like the other Liberators he'd seen in that he was dressed in grey. Tall. Muscular. Very well built.

Only...

There was something different about this bloke to the others he'd seen.

He had a smile on his face.

A smirk on his face.

He wasn't quite as dead in the eyes as the others he'd seen.

He looked like he still had a bit of *life* to him.

Outside, he could hear more gunshots. Less frequent, but still popping off. Those cries of pain were impossible to ignore. And the smell in the air even stronger now his cell door was open. The smell of smoke. Of burning.

Everything they'd built, everything they'd worked towards, burning to the ground.

But right now, at this moment, selfish as it sounded... the only thing that mattered was Steve.

Dad.

"So this is how it is, is it?" Billy asked. "You come in. You slaughter our people. You pretend you're doing it for some greater good. But you just can't resist some good old fashioned power tripping."

The Liberator shook his head. Smirked. Pushed the rifle closer to Steve's head. "Found this one crawling through the reception area. Said he was desperate to find somebody. His son."

Billy looked down at Steve and felt a lump in his throat. He realised something, then. Steve wasn't just beaten and bruised. He was bleeding. Badly.

Gunshot wounds, by the looks of things.

His right side.

His right leg.

Bleeding, a pool of blood all over the cell floor.

Billy went cold. "You—you bastards."

"I didn't want him to die alone," the Liberator said. "See, my friends, they can be ruthless. They can be savage. But... but, well, I don't know. Sometimes I remember. And it makes everything much harder."

"Remember what?"

"That you're... that you're people."

Billy shook his head. "What's that supposed to mean?"

The Liberator's smile dropped. He lowered his head. And Billy saw another side to him now.

He saw a man conflicted.

A man torn.

Torn in two directions.

"I'm not... I'm not supposed to tell you this. But my name is Tristan."

"I don't give a fuck what your name is. Let us go. Let me go, and let... let him go too. It's not too late to do the right thing."

"We *are* doing the right thing."

"By slaughtering communities? By wiping out entire towns? Butchering innocent people? You think that's the right thing?"

"We're... we're doing it in aid of something bigger. Something greater."

"You always are, you lot. That's always your excuse."

"You won't understand. You wouldn't. But... but future generations will. And when they look back in history at what we did—at the sacrifices we made—they'll thank us for it."

Billy stood there, and he legitimately did not know what the fuck to say. He just worried about Steve. 'Cause Steve wasn't in a good way. He really wasn't in a fucking good way at all.

"And what will they thank you for?" Billy asked.

Tristan held his ground. Kept his rifle pointed at Steve. His eyes wide. "For unity."

Billy had so many fucking questions he didn't know where to start.

But as much as he wanted answers, what mattered more was Steve.

Making sure he was okay.

Making sure he *survived*.

Because right now... Billy had to admit he was growing worried.

He was growing very fucking worried.

"Look," Billy said. "I don't know why you're doing what you're doing. I'd love to hear your full arguments behind your twisted logic, but frankly, I—I don't have the time. And neither does... neither does Steve. I won't go as far as saying you're a decent man. But you brought him here. You brought him to me. So there must be something inside you, however hidden it is. Some empathy. Some understanding. So, please. Let us go. Let us get the help we need. What are two extra survivors, really? What problem are we going to be to you?"

Tristan's hands shook. He shook his head, side to side. His eyes were wider than ever now, windows to his tortured soul. "I have orders."

"You don't always have to follow orders. You... you have to do what's right. And you know what's right. Surely you know what's right."

Tristan shook his head. He kept his rifle pointed at Steve, who lay there, struggling, writhing. He muttered something to himself under his breath.

And then he lifted his rifle.

Pointed it at Billy.

"I brought him here so you could die together. So... so he wouldn't be alone. I'm sorry... I'm sorry you're losing someone. But I promise, in time, it will be a worthy sacrifice. In time, it will be—"

"There's children here," Billy said.

Tristan's face turned red, just a little.

"Kids," Billy said. "Kids who'll never see their parents again. Kids who'll hide and then find themselves in a world where they're forced to survive. To do awful things. Awful, unimaginable fucking things. And that's not making for a better world. For a more united world. You're creating an entire generation of trauma. Of hatred. And they won't forgive you."

Tristan stood still. Speechless.

"I was one of those children once," Billy said. Lips quivering. "But I... I found my way out. Against all fucking odds, I found my way out. But I almost didn't. I got lost along the way far too many times. And you know what? Who can fucking blame me after what I went through?"

"Stop talking," Tristan said.

"But I realised I couldn't keep letting the past define me. I had to... I had to be better *now*. To see the good in people. To trust people more. Because... because not trusting people and not seeing the good in people. That's what's held me back. That's what's caused so much mess. And... and we don't always get it right. Sometimes, we trust the wrong people. But that's a risk we've got to take in life."

Tristan stood still. Rifle shaking more than ever right now.

He stood over Steve's bleeding body.

And a tear crept down his face.

"I'll never forgive you for this," Billy said. "I'll never forgive your people for this. But that shouldn't stop you from doing what's right."

Tristan lowered his head. He took in a deep, shaky breath. Looked like he was deep in thought for quite some time.

And then he looked back up at Billy.

"I don't expect your forgiveness," he said.

And then he started walking away.

Back towards the cell door.

Grabbed that cell door.

And for a second, Billy thought he knew how this was going down.

He was going to slam that door shut and trap the pair of them in here to die together.

But instead... he stopped.

Stood at the door.

"I don't expect your forgiveness," he repeated. "But I expect you to walk out of here and to never come back. I expect you to find somewhere solitary and isolated for yourself. And if our paths cross ever again... I expect you to understand things won't go as well for you."

He stepped away from the door.

And he walked out of the cell.

Billy stood there.

Heart racing.
Gunshots echoing outside.
Tristan's footsteps walking down into the police station.
And Steve, lying there, gasping before him.
He didn't know how he'd done it, but he'd done it.
The Liberator was gone.
And they had a chance.

CHAPTER FORTY-FOUR

Billy rushed over to Steve's side.

Steve was in a bad way. Blood all over the cell floor, seeping through Billy's jeans and onto his knees. He could hear gunshots outside, but they were fading and growing more infrequent. He could hear cries, too, but they were weakening, too—an ominous and horrendous sign to contemplate.

He crouched over Steve, and he wanted to comfort him, he wanted to get him out of here, he wanted to get *both* of them out of here.

But that voice in his head told him it was already too late.

No.

He couldn't think that way.

He had to try.

"Come on," Billy said, reaching down and trying to lift Steve up. "We can get out of here. We've done it. We've—we've made it."

But when Billy grabbed Steve, he let out a wince. Let out a pained cry. It was so bad that it made Billy stop. Made him let go. He didn't want to hurt him. Not more than he was already hurting.

"I'm sorry," Billy said. "I—I know you're hurting. But we really need to get out of here. We might not get another chance."

He went to lift Steve again, knowing full well he was going to protest, knowing full well he was suffering.

And then he felt that gasp again.

The whimper again.

Childlike.

And he felt the warm blood trickling out over his fingers.

He lowered Steve back down. Couldn't hold on to him when he was hurting like this. Didn't want to do any more damage than had already been done.

But then... what *could* he do?

Was there anything he could do?

He wasn't sure.

He didn't know.

He just knew he had a chance, and he had to get out of here.

"Come on," Billy said. "Help me out here, you stubborn git. Don't go giving up on me now."

He went to lift him again when suddenly, Steve grabbed his arm.

He grabbed it and held it tight at first. And looked right up into Billy's eyes with a lucidity that Billy hadn't seen from Steve in a long time.

"I'm—I'm sorry," Steve said.

Billy frowned. "Sorry for what?"

"For doubting... For thinking you..."

Billy nodded. "I would've thought I'd done it if I were in your shoes, too. Don't beat yourself up about it. But yeah. Bit of a dick move."

Steve laughed a little, and it made him wince again, made him cry out.

And it made Billy realise even more that they needed to get out of here.

Because Tristan had already told him if they ran into each other again, the outcome wouldn't be as positive for Billy.

But as he crouched there, Steve holding on to his arm with his shaking, gradually loosening hand, he had a strange feeling. A strange sense that this was only going in one direction. That there was only going to be one outcome here.

No.

That didn't have to be right.

That didn't have to be true.

But as he crouched there, telling himself he was going to get out of here, that they were *both* going to get out of here... he wasn't moving. He wasn't trying anything.

He was just watching.

Breathing with Steve.

Letting him hold his arm as blood pooled out underneath him.

And he didn't want to accept where he thought this conversation was going.

He didn't want to accept where he thought this moment was going.

But it felt like both of them understood as they sat there in the silence.

"You know what you have to do this time, Billy," Steve said.

Billy lowered his head, and he closed his eyes. He felt stinging tears building up in his eyes. He knew what Steve was saying. He knew what he was implying.

And he didn't want to accept it.

He wanted to fight it.

He wanted to run from it.

But he knew, deep down, there was no running from it this time.

"I can't leave you," Billy said.

"You can," Steve said before coughing and spluttering blood. "You... you can because... you can because you know you have to. You can because... because you have before. You have before because... because you've realised you're strong enough. You always have been strong enough."

Billy crouched there, looking down into Steve's eyes, shaking his head. And he felt like a kid again. A lost kid who needed something. Who needed *someone*.

"I don't think I can do this alone," Billy said.

"Eastbrook... Eastbrook needs you. The people... the people out there. The other communities. They... they all need you. And they need you more than I do right now."

He heard these words, and he felt that sense of responsibility weighing on his shoulders, and he shook his head.

Because he didn't want to face up to that responsibility.

He didn't want to accept that responsibility.

He didn't want to accept what it meant.

But at the same time... he knew what he had to do.

He knew Steve was right.

As painful and as gut-wrenching as it was, Steve was right.

"I love you, Dad," Billy said.

A tear rolled down Steve's face. A smile tugged at his lips. He took in a sharp breath, which sounded painful, laboured. And he squeezed Billy's arm tightly for just a second. "I love you too, son. I just wish... I just wish I'd got to spend... to spend more time with you. Growing up. And..."

Billy thought about the childhood he'd had.

The trauma he'd had.

Not just at the hands of Ramiro and his people.

But at the hands of the man he used to call Dad.

A small part of him did feel betrayed that he'd been left to suffer the fate he'd suffered.

But that wasn't on Steve.

That wasn't anyone's fault but the man responsible.

The *men* responsible.

"I'm just grateful I got to spend the time with you that I did. And that I got to know."

"Got to... to know what?"

"To know that you were my dad. Because—because it's the best thing I've ever discovered. Even if I did think you were a bit of a weirdo at first."

Steve—Dad—laughed again.

And then he spluttered, descending into a painful and bloody coughing fit.

And as Billy crouched there beside him, cell door open, knowing full well anyone could just wander in and take him out any second now... he held on to Dad's arm.

"Ssh," Billy said. "It'll be okay. It's—it's going to be okay."

He held on to Dad's arm, and he felt his grip loosening.

He heard his breathing growing raspier.

He looked down at him through tearful eyes, and he saw him fading right before his eyes.

"Fight for... fight for these people," Steve said. "Fight for... for everyone."

Billy tightened his grip. "I will, Dad. I will."

Steve closed his eyes.

Took in a deep breath and let it go, blood bubbles expanding from his nostrils.

"Fight for..." he started.

And then his words turned into an exhalation.

A raspy exhalation.

His hand went totally numb.

And as much as Billy waited, that inhalation didn't come.

Steve was gone.

Dad was gone.

CHAPTER FORTY-FIVE

Billy stepped out of his cell and tried to hold his head up high.

He stood there in the police station corridor. It was dark in here. He could hear gunshots outside still, popping away. Screaming, but far less frequent now. He knew the Liberators would've finished storming through Eastbrook at this point. And based on everything Meg told him, there wouldn't be many survivors at all.

But as he stood there in the corridor, he prayed there were survivors.

One. Two. Three.

Enough.

Enough to spread the word about the sins of the Liberators.

And enough to form a group that could rise up and fight back against them.

Stop their genocide, once and for all.

He thought about Steve. Dying in his arms. He thought about the promise he'd made him. The promise to fight for this community. To fight for everyone.

He felt that responsibility weighing down on his shoulders.

And he took a deep breath.

He was going to fight.

He wasn't going to let Steve down.

"I won't let you down," Billy said. "I'll never stop fighting."

He went to walk down the corridor when he heard something behind him.

Banging.

Banging against one of the cell doors.

He walked over to it. Frowning.

Stepped right up to it.

Opened the hatch and looked inside.

When he saw who was staring back at him, he never thought he'd say this, but he felt majorly fucking relieved.

"Marco," Billy said.

"You gonna just stand there? Or are you gonna get me out?"

Billy nodded.

He walked back to his cell.

Back to the door.

Yanked the keys out of the lock, then rushed back down to Marco's cell, fully aware the Liberators could return at any moment.

He stuck the key in the door.

Turned it.

Opened the door.

"Shit," Marco said. Shaking. "Started to think nobody was gonna come for me."

"Well, you're in luck. Only... not really."

Marco nodded. "Figured that much from the explosions. How bad is it?"

Billy walked down the corridor, past the holding cells, towards the reception area. "I haven't seen for myself yet. But I'm guessing pretty bad."

They walked across the reception area.

Stood at the doors.

Billy held on to the handle and looked around at Marco, who nodded back at him.

"Here goes nothing," Billy said.

He opened the doors.

A gust of wind blew into the reception area of the police station.

The smell of smoke thick in the air.

And the taste.

The unmistakable metallic taste of death.

Billy saw bodies lying in the streets.

He saw blood everywhere.

He saw people lying there, totally dead, face down.

Men.

Women.

Children.

And he saw survivors, too.

People dragging themselves through the streets, missing limbs.

He saw children peeking out of broken windows, tears in their eyes.

He saw the bullets on the ground, and he heard the eerie silence hanging over his home, as the misty skies made everything seem even more... hellish...

And then he remembered Steve's words.

Fight for these people.

Fight for everyone.

He stood there, and he saw the few survivors of his community.

The dead far outnumbering them.

He thought of Marco, standing by his side.

He thought about Rex.

Waiting at home.

At least, he hoped.

And he thought of Faye, too.

Even in her betrayal... he thought of Faye.

"Shit," Marco said. "More of 'em."

Billy turned around, and he saw something that made his stomach sink.

In the distance, heading towards the community, worming their way in through an exploded gap in the wall that these people had spent so long building, he saw more Liberators.

Their grey uniforms.

The rifles in their hands.

All walking in unison.

A death machine, getting closer and closer.

"What're we gonna do now?" Marco asked.

Billy tightened his fists.

And this time, he felt pain there. Pain from the stab wounds.

But he didn't luxuriate in that pain anymore.

He didn't sink into it and use it as a distraction.

Instead, he thought about the pain of the rest of his community.

The rest of his people.

And the pain of so many people out there in the world who would suffer at the hands of these monsters.

He remembered Steve's words in the garden when they were drinking a beer that day—a day that felt so long ago, now.

Sometimes leaders aren't the ones you expect.

He took a deep breath, and he stared at that oncoming force, marching right towards his home.

"We're going to fight for our people," Billy said. "We're going to fight for everyone. And we're going to destroy these Liberators. No matter what it takes."

END OF BOOK 11

End of Darkness, the twelfth (and final!) book in the Survive the Darkness series, is now available.

If you want to be notified when Ryan Casey's next novel is released—and receive an exclusive post apocalyptic novel totally free—sign up for the author newsletter: ryancaseybooks.com/fanclub